IMMO

Immortal Beloved

A novelization by
James Ellison

Based on a screenplay by
Bernard Rose

HEADLINE

The right of James Ellison to be identified as the Author of
the Work based on the screenplay by Bernard Rose
has been asserted by him in accordance with the
Copyright, Designs and Patents Act 1988.

First published in Great Britain in 1995
by HEADLINE BOOK PUBLISHING

10 9 8 7 6 5 4 3 2 1

ISBN 0 7472 5141 X

Typeset by Keyboard Services, Luton, Beds

Printed and bound in Great Britain by
Cox & Wyman Ltd, Reading, Berks

HEADLINE BOOK PUBLISHING
A division of Hodder Headline PLC
338 Euston Road
London NW1 3BH

Contents

Prelude

In his final hours Ludwig van Beethoven lapsed into a coma and his laboured breathing, which had daily grown worse, became an honest and true death rattle. He lay abed in his chamber, his abdomen swollen and his once-stocky frame little more than a sack of bones. Never handsome, his face was now an ashen veil worn by a soul the world admired but of which it knew little. It was five o'clock in the afternoon, the twenty-sixth of March, 1827.

He had been ill since December, when, after quarrelling with his brother Johann, he had returned to Vienna in an open carriage. He had caught a chill. A fever had set in. He began to vomit and his intestines, which during the course of his life had given him nothing but trouble – indeed, he believed they had ruined his hearing – racked him with agony. His feet swelled. His skin turned a ghastly shade of yellow as jaundice set in. Three times he was operated on to drain his abdomen

1

bloated with dropsy. Dr Warwuch ordered herbs which were quite useless, while his old friend, the Italian physician Malfatti, prescribed iced punch. But all to no avail. By the time some fine Mosel wine arrived, requested from Schott's many weeks before, Beethoven could only say, 'Pity, pity ... too late.'

Those were his last words.

It was altogether fitting, given Beethoven's stormy nature, that outside as the end grew near, the sky darkened early, a storm came up with a harsh north wind, and snow began to fall. And as he lay abed scarcely conscious of the physical wreckage his body had been reduced to, he seemed to become aware of the storm that raged outside. After a series of lightning flashes illuminated the night sky, he raised his right hand and clenched his fist. It was as though his dying vision could glimpse behind the faltering eyelids nature's rage enfolding his own. But it was certain that he could not hear the thunder. The greatest composer the world had ever known was totally deaf.

He had long ago told himself: *For thee there is no longer any happiness except in thyself, in thy art*. And so he had lived, much of his life, without love – a domestic life as disordered as it was shabby. Yet he had spoken confidentially, even towards the end, of a woman whom he had known intimately but once, a woman he claimed to have loved more than life itself, and about whom he had written these words: *Nevertheless it is now as on the first day*.

The world has never learned, with certainty, her identity, though the candidates have been scrutinized for over a century. Of one we can say – a fact long suppressed, but it can now be recorded here – that as

Beethoven lay dying, she came to his bedside. He called her his Immortal Beloved.

> *Can you change the fact that you are not wholly mine — I not wholly yours? O, Lord, gaze at beautiful nature, and resign yourself to what must be. Love demands everything and rightly so; and thus it is for me with you, and for you with me.*

So he had written long ago. Whether he could sense, at the end, her redemptive presence, we will never know. In his rooms on the third floor of an old convent of Spanish monks, called the *Schwarzspanierhaus*, Beethoven died just before six o'clock in the evening.

Chapter 1

A Letter in a Desk

Anton Schindler, the man closest to Ludwig van Beethoven in his final years, who had given his heart and soul to the great man, returned to the *Schwarzspanierhaus* within minutes of the funeral. Notwithstanding his hurried departure, the funeral was a grand affair. It was attended by upwards of thirty thousand people, the highest and lowest of Viennese society, who had come to pay homage to one of the world's mightiest composers. However, it was also true, as one bystander said, that Vienna loves a good funeral. On a mild spring afternoon the coffin had been borne by eight singers from the Imperial Opera, who sang the chorale from *Wilhelm Tell* and carried him through the streets from his home to the church. There were many torchbearers, and a solemn choir performed his own *Miserere mei Deus* accompanied by trombones. Following the service the procession moved to the cemetery in the suburb of Wahring, Beethoven's body resting in a magnificent hearse drawn by four white horses. And there he was consecrated to the earth.

But no sooner was the coffin lowered and the torches extinguished than Schindler shouldered his way to the crowd's periphery. He was suddenly anxious, his heart hammering; he broke out in perspiration. It was the thought of what was bound to happen at the house that troubled him, and this dignified man in his dark frock coat literally broke into a run. Reaching his coach, he insisted that the surprised tippler he had hired use his whip. All the way back through the streets of Vienna he heard the horses' hooves clattering against the counterpoint of his beating heart, and he strained to calm the fear that he might arrive, even now, too late. He recalled the eulogy:

He was a musician, but also a man, a man in every sense, in the highest sense. Because he shut himself off from the world, they called him hostile.

Schindler had seen them all there, following the coffin like himself – Beethoven's closest friends and admirers, with whom indeed his relations had been difficult, sometimes brutal.

They said he was unfeeling and called him callous. But he was not hard of heart. It is the finest blades that are most easily blunted, bent, or broken. He fled because he did not find, in the whole of his loving nature, a weapon to protect himself from the world.

Following the coffin was Countess Anna Marie

Erdody, the sad eccentric Hungarian whom Beethoven had once loved. And, weeping copiously, Countess Julia Gallenburg walked beside her husband, the hopelessly stupid Count Gallenburg. Even Johanna was there, Beethoven's widowed sister-in-law, with whom he had battled ceaselessly over the custody of his nephew – her son – Karl. Poor Karl.

He withdrew from his fellow men after he had given them everything and had received nothing in return. He lived alone because he found no second self.

It was all true, all tragic.

And all the dates, all the moments and compositions of his lifetime, the stark outlines of the man's biography, could give no real hint of the man's staggering genius:

Born in Bonn in 1770 ... arrived in cosmopolitan Vienna in 1792, the musical capital of the Hapsburg Empire ... Soon well known as a superb virtuoso of the newly invented piano ... Composer of nine symphonies, seven concertos, one opera, seventeen string quartets, fifteen sonatas ... The power of his compositions became the measure of all classical music, an expression of the Enlightenment, and opened the way to a new romanticism. In a single decade, beginning in 1803, his prodigous hand cast a heroic vision of mankind, and as his life drew near its end he captured the idealism of the Enlightenment in the great Ninth Symphony.

No such simple lineaments could encompass the man's hold on the imagination of his generation.

After what seemed an eternity the coach drew up before the *Schwarzspanierhaus*. Schindler sprang out of the coach and tossed the driver the equivalent of a dozen mugs in a beer house. He entered the Convent and bounded up the great staircase. He arrived at the top of the stairs panting, his side aching, but halted only a moment to catch his breath before entering the apartment.

'*Meister!*'

He cried out the words, as he often had, despite the unalterable fact of Beethoven's death. And as he moved through the apartment he added, beneath his breath, 'It's *Papageno!*' – Beethoven's pet name for him.

His first objective was to make certain that no one but himself was there. He walked through the ante-chamber and the entrance hall, poking his head into the music room. In the bedroom, where the stench of illness and perfumed medications lingered, he paused. He had heard that in the hours after death the Danhausers had come to make a death mask before Beethoven's body was put into a coffin. Indeed, the floor was littered with chunks of dried plaster. What artifice, immortality! Schindler crushed some clumps to dust before continuing through, checking even the servant's room and the kitchen before finally coming to the composing room.

Nobody.

He gave a sigh of relief and felt a loosening of tension deep within himself. He was the first. Which was not to say he had forever to set about his business. But there was something of the greatest importance which he had to search out before anyone else arrived.

Schindler – Beethoven's loyal factotum – was thirty-one years old, aged beyond his years, and bespectacled, with a gaze at once steely and wounded. A man with uses that went far beyond his admiration for the master, and which had bound Beethoven to him like no other. Born in Moravia, he had become first violinist of the theatre in der Josephstadt in Vienna, and directed the orchestra at the Karntrerthor. Four years earlier, in 1823, he had performed every one of Beethoven's symphonies under the direction of the master himself. But what was more, he was a lawyer, or, more accurately, he had studied the law. He knew what a tort was. He was capable of handling practical matters such as paying bills and keeping a ledger – abilities as foreign and as puzzling to Beethoven as the tramontanes of Tibet. Not even Schindler's assistance, however, had prevented the music room from becoming a thorough mess in Beethoven's last years, overflowing with papers, sketchbooks, and bundles of scores. The two pianos were swamped, the desk was covered. Schindler shook his head at the chaos, but there was no time to straighten up the mess, only to wade into it. He set to work.

Someday, he thought with resolution, and soon, he would need to comb meticulously through all of this. The manuscripts must be put in order, the letters catalogued. Several shelves were filled to overflowing with the master's conversation books – some four hundred of them – in which Beethoven's visitors had recorded their remarks. One day these would have to be pored over carefully. Schindler took one volume in his hands and leafed through it. He considered taking the whole load with him to his rooms, even tonight, because he knew that the cleansing must take place at once so that the books did not fall into some bibliophile's hands – and then into history. The prospect of that did not please Schindler.

He knew that history's pursuit of Beethoven's life must be handled with extreme care. Had not the master, while on his deathbed, said to him, in witness of Stephan von Breuning, pointing to his papers, 'Gather them up and make the best use of them, but the strict truth in everything. I make you both responsible.'

The strict truth, did not mean, so far as either Beethoven or Anton Schindler was concerned, the truth covered with warts. What if it fell to him, *Papageno*, to write the biography of Beethoven? It surely would not mean that certain ghastly facets of the master need be brought to light. Everyone in Vienna knew Beethoven was a strange and unusually difficult man. Throughout the royal courts of Europe he was known to be an eccentric and even, at times, an unpleasant person. But who would ever forgive the biographer who wrote that the man who recast humankind through his music detested so many of his fellow men, could not live with a servant or barely be trusted to empty his own chamber pot? That he was a man who lay abed wretched and woebegone if two days passed without an admiring letter? That he was a man who cynically used others, and that there were women he frequented who were no better than harlots? But those were not truths; they were a form of scandal-mongering, and Schindler knew he must do all he could to prevent such a travesty from happening. He had been named Beethoven's executor, and the truth of the master's life would have to answer to him.

And it was in that spirit, with a frenzied sense of mission, that Anton Schindler began riffling through the papers of his late employer, Ludwig van Beethoven, on the day that he was buried. He looked first of all for what he knew would intrigue him most.

Beethoven's testament.

He did not find it – or, rather, he did, but not soon enough. Schindler searched every nook and cranny, in a race against time. He had not eaten and was plagued by a headache, but he kept at it, rummaging through the papers with a growing frustration that culminated when he heard steps on the landing. He knew with whom he would have to contend. A moment later the door burst open.

'*Bravo*, Herr Schindler! On the job as always. Not one to let the grass grow under your feet.'

Karl Holz stood before him. Schindler's nemesis. The second violinist with the Schuppanzigh quartet. Beethoven had liked him, had considered him talented; Schindler knew this and had had to swallow the truth without letting the bitterness contaminate his love for the master. Indeed, all the bitterness he might have felt for Beethoven flowed instead on to this decent man who happened by chance to be a slanderer and a drunk and who stood before him now with funeral crepes hanging from his coat, applauding with more than a touch of irony.

'It was a noble eulogy, Herr Schindler! You have a way with words.'

Schindler said nothing. Instead he continued his search.

'Return to your homes, then,' cried Holz, quoting the

eulogy in some loose approximation, 'in sorrow but composed. And whenever, during your lives, the power of his works overwhelms one like a crashing blow—'

'*Storm*,' said Schindler, hiding his annoyance, standing to his full height. He continued quietly, saying, '*Crashing storm. When the rapture pours out in the midst of a generation yet unborn; then remember this hour and think: we were there when they buried him, and when he died we wept!*'

'Extinguish the torches!' cried Holz, and he burst out laughing. 'A noble eulogy. Quite up to the gravity of the occasion. Which reminds me: Ludwig often spoke of your gift for flattery. And he was quite right.'

Ludwig indeed, thought Schindler.

'But I should imagine,' said Holz, 'that more than adulation, a testament is now what occupies your thoughts.'

Schindler glared at him. 'And yours?' he said.

'I have come with Johann.'

'Ah.'

'The will should be found with the money,' said Holz. 'The Maestro never let those banknotes out of his sight.'

'And I imagine,' said Schindler, 'that Johann is looking for it too.' As he talked he continued to plough through the piles of papers.

A moment later Johann Beethoven, the eminent pharmacist, rushed into the room, crying, 'Do you have it, Schindler? Have you found his papers?'

In a fever of excitement and nervousness, Beethoven's youngest brother pushed his way past Holz. Schindler regarded him coolly. Johann had a face like the prow of a slaveship with pince-nez for a mast.

'No,' he said. And continued looking.

12

'Perhaps it's been taken,' said Holz good-naturedly, laughing as he uncapped a flask.

Johann looked from one to the other, regarding both Holz and Schindler with distrust. At last he asked, 'Which one of you is the thief?' He rushed up to Schindler. 'Produce the money, or I will have you arrested!'

'Arrest me,' said Schindler. 'By all means.' He continued to look through the desk, which he had already searched.

Johann's frustration was understandable to both Schindler and Holz. Where at least they both enjoyed ties of amity to Beethoven, Johann was merely his brother. Schindler knew that Johann Beethoven considered himself to be a kind, honest and decent man; in the wake of his famous brother's death, he wanted a final expression of filial love, in the form of banknotes. Wanted it desperately. That Johann was already a wealthy landowner was beside the point, Schindler supposed. Especially if you were the brother of a man who could not bear to pronounce your name, who called you 'brother Cain' and 'my ass of a brother' and 'brain eater' when he called you anything at all.

'I took him in,' said Johann testily, 'when nobody, but nobody, could bear his company.'

Schindler could not suppress a laugh. 'And now you want to be paid, eh?'

He had noticed in the desk a small hidden drawer. He tried to force it but without success. When he moved around to examine the back of the desk he found a protruding nail. He extracted it and pulled off the back panel. A bundle wrapped in a ribbon fell to the floor. As Schindler bent to pick it up, he could feel both Johann and Holz breathing down his neck. 'Bank shares,' he observed.

'Give that to me!' cried Johann. He struggled inside his greatcoat for a document which he removed and brandished in front of Schindler's face. 'Here it is! I have his will!'

Schindler didn't move. He knew more or less what was coming as Johann read, '"I declare my brothers, Caspar and Johann, to be the heirs to my fortune, if it can so be called."'

'Nonsense,' said Schindler. 'That was written twenty-five years ago.'

Johann held up the paper. 'As Caspar is long dead, that leaves me. Just me. Give me my money!'

Schindler tore open the letter with the bank shares. It, too, contained a will – written, barely legibly, in the hand of the dying man. It was scrawled across a single page, and dated three days earlier.

Schindler read it aloud:

'"*All my music and all the capital of my estate shall go to my sole heir ... my Immortal Beloved!*"'

Schindler looked up. Neither Johann or Holz had moved a muscle nor said a word. Finally, Johann said with a sneer, 'Now just who is this Immortal Beloved person? What nonsense! Ludwig had lost his senses.'

'And it is signed,' said Schindler, holding up the letter for both men to see. 'Ludwig van Beethoven.'

'This is some foul joke,' said Johann acidly.

'There is something more.'

Bound with this testament and the banknotes was a letter addressed in Beethoven's younger, steadier hand, the paper now old and yellowed. Schindler held it up as well; the seal had been broken, and he opened it carefully.

'What is my brother up to?' asked Johann. He tapped his foot nervously.

Schindler read the address, which was unfamiliar to him. Johann snatched the letter from his hands but he, too, was perplexed. At the address, his eyes shot up, and he fumed, 'Absurd!' Schindler took it back.

Holz tipped his flask up for another swallow, smiled and said, 'Come now, don't keep me in suspense. What does it say?'

'Nothing,' said Johann.

'That is not so,' said Schindler.

'The letter bears no name,' Johann insisted.

But it was in Beethoven's unmistakable hand and, in fact, had been written in one of his states of great passion; the elegant letters were scrawled across the page. Schindler found himself reading aloud:

'"*To my immortal Beloved . . .*"'

Chapter 2

The Immortal Beloved

'What?' Holz, who was no longer laughing, peered over Schindler's shoulder and began to read:

"My angel, my all, my other self, just a few words today and that in pencil (yours)..."

He glanced at Schindler and exclaimed incredulously, 'Ah! The maestro nursing a secret passion!'

'There is no date,' said Schindler, turning over each page of the letter.

'It is timeless,' said Holz, sarcastically, but then adding as a self-reproach, 'Bah!'

Schindler moved away from Holz and continued reading. The words struck him hard, one by one, as he heard Beethoven's voice pronounce them, and his incomprehension gave way to a sense of shock, even wonder. He was saying without thinking, 'I never heard such sentiment from his lips.'

'Nor I,' said Holz. 'Though he had Peters' wife on loan and Frau—'

'You are disgusting,' cried Schindler. Although certainly not untrue, he thought.

Going back in his mind over the last decade since he met Beethoven, Schindler had heard not a single breath of rumour of a sentimental relation, nothing of love. But that was in Beethoven's old age and surely did not represent the tremendous breadth of his life. When he was young he had had many love affairs with ardent countesses, or so it was generally assumed. And he was, after all, the composer of the *Moonlight Sonata* and many other works which were evidently full of the awareness and appreciation of profound, enduring love...

'This must be a letter from his youth,' he decided aloud.

'It is nothing,' said Johann acidly. 'It means nothing. Let us be done with such nonsense.'

'Not so fast,' said Schindler.

He began to read aloud:

'"Why this deep grief when necessity speaks? Can our love subsist, except by sacrifices, by not asking everything? Can you change the fact that you are not wholly mine – I not wholly yours? O, Lord, gaze at beautiful nature, and resign yourself to what must be. Love demands everything and rightly so; and thus it is for me with you, and for you with me. Only you so easily forget that I must live for both you and me. If we were wholly united, you would feel the pain as little as I do."'

'What does that mean?' asked Johann. '"*Feel the pain as little as I do?*"'

'Where was it written?' said Holz.

'It bears the word Karlsbad,' Schindler answered. 'When was Beethoven in Bohemia?'

'He was there in 1806,' Johann replied. 'It was the same year that Caspar married. I remember, because Ludwig was furious about the marriage when he returned. And perhaps he was there later, I don't know. He seldom made his whereabouts known to me.'

The letter was strange, not only for existing at all – was it ever sent? How did it come to be among Beethoven's effects? – but because of its tone of truly anguished love.

'"*My journey was a fearful one; I did not reach here until 4 o'clock yesterday morning. Lacking horses the postcoach chose another route, but what an awful one; at the stage before the last I was warned not to travel at night; I was made fearful of a forest, but that only made me the more eager – and I was wrong. The coach must needs break down on the wretched road, a bottomless mud road.*"'

An anecdote with the shape of his love life.

The letter was in several parts, Schindler realized. In the evening of the same day, Beethoven had added a post-script; Schindler began reading again:

'"*You are suffering – Ah, wherever I am, you are*

with me – I will arrange it with you and me that I can live with you."'

'Beethoven? Live with a woman?' cried Johann. 'Pity's be. Nothing is more unlikely.'

'"Much as you love me – I love you more. But do not ever conceal yourself from me ... Good night ... Oh God ... So near! So far! Is not our love a truly heavenly structure, and also as firm as the vault of Heaven?"'

Schindler put down the letter and said to himself rather than to Holz and Johann, 'Who could this be?'

'The only love he held was for himself.'

This remark – not exactly an answer – came from Therese, Johann's wife, who, as chance would have it, now stood in the doorway, ill-tempered as ever, her lips screwed into one of her most horrible expressions.

'I suffered his insults and his temper,' she continued, as a shrew persists its burrowing. 'I suffered in silence when he spat the food I prepared back in my face.'

A big, lumbering woman with thick lips and a look of spoiled sumptuousness, she moved towards her husband. Schindler had to admit to himself that he shared Beethoven's distaste for the apothecary's wife. She had come into Johann's life as his housekeeper and found her way into his bed as something else. The brothers had come to furious blows over Johann's relationship with her, which Beethoven found lacking in moral fibre – indeed, stinking of immorality not to mention greed. And now she meant to take a measure of revenge.

'I turned the other way when he spread lies about me and Johann,' she cried. 'And five months ago I said nothing when he yelled at me as I swabbed his bedsores. Why? Because I thought he was not like us. He was a great man. A great composer. The whole world proclaimed his genius. Who was I to say different? But we did what no *beloved* would do, and I tell you one thing: That money is ours.'

'It is not,' said Schindler, adamantly waving the will in front of them.

For it was the combination of the letter and the will together that was so significant. The letter had been written long ago, and in isolation simply might be a curiosity for a future biographer. But discovered as it was, bound with the will, it assumed another, entirely different, meaning.

'We'll see to whom this belongs,' Schindler said, a note of finality in his voice.

Defiantly, he bound the will with the banknotes and the letter. He moved towards the door. Schindler wanted to be done with these people. The master was dead, and although the factotum had hoped throughout the long illness that the end would relieve him of a tremendous burden, it was not to be. Perhaps it would have been so if Beethoven were a relation, an ordinary mother or father – someone mortal who would die like all mortal men to be grieved over and then forgotten. But now, the magnitude of Beethoven's passing struck him. He felt his own insignificance more acutely in the presence of these petty souls for whom the stench of greed overwhelmed the lingering odour of death. The death, furthermore, of a genius. Johann intercepted him at the door.

'It no longer matters!' cried Johann, grabbing the lapels of Schindler's greatcoat, almost pleading. 'He is gone. Maybe for the best. We have the music. He belongs to ... the whole of mankind. Destroy that letter. It will only show his disordered life to the world.'

'This will is his dying wish,' said Schindler, as though preternaturally aware of the project hatching in his brain. 'We owe him at least the effort.'

Johann stomped his feet in frustration and anger. 'You have no authority in this matter!'

'I have *his* authority!' Schindler fired back.

'Still the faithful dog, eh?'

'He was my friend.'

'What friend would be so cruel?'

Schindler stopped and turned. 'And what brother so uncaring?'

He sensed that he had hurt Johann, hurt him to the quick, but as Johann regarded him evenly, the hurt in his eyes quickly turned to rage. 'You know *nothing* of my brother,' he shouted. 'You know nothing at all.'

The words followed Schindler as he descended the stairs and remained with him as he hailed a coach. He sat within it, burning still, with an explosive mixture of pride and shame applied to his honest and eternally decent soul.

Chapter 3

An Incident in Karlsbad

And so it came about that Anton Schindler set out, within days of the funeral, to discover the identity of Beethoven's Immortal Beloved. In principle there was much left to do in the way of settling the master's estate, but it could all wait. To embark on such a journey was, for Schindler, a way of keeping the master alive within him. For he knew that everyone should be finally as lucky as he, to have been touched by the life of a genius. If swabbing bed-sores was the least of what one had to put up with, so be it. The letter was in his hand as he climbed into the fiacre and cried to the coachman, 'Take me to Karlsbad.'

My angel, my all, my other self...

He read and reread the letter with a clear eye on the way. He memorized its contents in the hope that the secrets and allusions it contained might lead him to the identity of the recipient, if indeed the recipient – this

Immortal Beloved – were not merely a made-up creature of Beethoven's roiled brain.

> *Just a few words today and that in pencil (yours) ... only tomorrow will I know for certain where I am to stay, a worthless waste of time and such – why this deep sorrow where necessity speaks? ...Can you do anything to alter the fact that you are not wholly mine – I not wholly yours?*

It had not fallen to Anton Schindler – and it was all the more reason he was intrigued – to know anything coherent and solid on the sentimental life of the master. Certainly nothing, in any event, if by that was meant attachments of *consequence* with women. The Beethoven whom Schindler had known was frequently ill and always irascible, save when those rare bolts of kindness struck from the blue, with no trace of contempt, when even a dash of irony was served up with affection.

It is your duty to attend my house at 2 o'clock tomorrow afternoon, at which time, after partaking of bread and water, you will be placed under arrest for the duration of twenty-four hours.

That was often Beethoven's way with Schindler, and he had accepted such invitations and all they implied with gratitude and more than a trace of martyrdom. He had heard rumours of Beethoven's relations with women, but the discovery of this letter addressed to his Immortal Beloved was like the unearthing of an ancient city lost to volcanic ash.

*Love demands everything and quite rightly so;
that is how I feel towards you and you towards me.
Only you so readily forget that I must live for me and
for you ...*

The date of the letter was uncertain – Johann had
suggested 1806 or thereabouts – and it appeared to have
been sent to a room at the Swan Hotel in Karlsbad.
However, the greater mystery remained: Beethoven
rarely made fair copies of his correspondence, and it
appeared that he must have recovered the original of
this particular letter, but why had it been returned to
him? Schindler could not tell. And of course by whom it
had been received, read and returned, Schindler had not
the slightest idea.

*Take courage! remain my true, my only treasure,
as I remain yours! The gods must send us the rest,
whatever has been ordained for us and must be.*

Schindler would, if it please those selfsame gods, find
out.

The Swan Hotel was a temple to leisure in the name of
good health, famed for its supply of medicinal salts of
mineral-water baths available in every possible way.
The hotel itself was a fine specimen of its kind, a four-
storey affair which looked magnificent in the summer,
when busy, rather than now in the midst of a harsh
early spring. But it was passably warm inside, and
behind the desk in the spare and elegant lobby stood an
old Bohemian woman.

She was round-faced and ruddy, with the gestures of

an owner and undoubtedly a widow, well able to size up a stranger for what he was or was not and could afford by the day, week, or month. She was, Schindler could tell, a businesswoman who liked business people, as well as nobles who were not destitute; but if nobility of purpose shined through in a man not entirely one or the other, and yet was cultivated, she could expect decency and provide generosity of spirit in return. Such a definition of character clearly fitted Schindler.

She said pleasantly, 'May I help you?'

'Good afternoon, Frau...'

'Streicher.'

He bowed. 'Herr Schindler.'

'Let me find your reservation.'

'I'm afraid I have arrived without one.'

'No matter. Always a room at the Swan for a gentleman such as yourself.'

'I would rather have the answer to a question,' he said as he took out the letter and, without thinking, asked, 'Do you know the name Ludwig van Beethoven?'

This was a question which, asked of anyone within the Empire possessed of the mildest form of intelligence, ought to have produced a warm assent. In this woman the notion that she didn't know of the master, however eccentric he might have been, should have engendered a form of delightful indignation; while the implication she might have heard his music, a touch of flattery. But nothing of the sort. Instead, almost with a sneer, she grunted, 'Are you talking about the composer?'

'Why, yes.'

'I knew him,' Frau Streicher said with a sniff.

'Did he ever stay here?'

She leaned towards Schindler and asked confidentially, 'Are you a policeman?'

Schindler shook his head. 'No.'

She puffed her lower lip with fake propriety. 'Then I will not answer you.'

'Please,' he implored, 'I am trying to conclude his affairs. It is my—'

'Are you saying that Beethoven is *dead*?'

'Alas,' said Schindler, sensing that she was more eager for gossip than shocked or sad at the news of his passing.

'Best thing for him,' asserted the old woman. 'A terrible man.'

'Then he stayed here!'

'Here? Yes, he certainly did stay here, and it's not soon to be forgotten.' She let out a wheezy sigh. 'It was a long time ago. I mainly recollect the damage.'

'The damage?'

'The damage I was never paid for.'

Schindler sensed an opening, and drew himself up. 'I find it difficult to understand what exactly he—'

'Well, he smashed everything,' snapped the woman, not giving him a chance to speak. 'Smashed it all up. I'll tell you how much . . .'

Schindler withdrew from his bag the bundle of bank notes. She noted the presence of money as she did her sums.

'There was the chair he broke like sticks for firewood, three florins. The window smashed, five. I had to paint the entire suite. And in addition—'

'Will this be sufficient?'

Frau Streicher's beady eyes focused on the bank notes Schindler peeled off before going back to her list. 'A whole new set of curtains,' she said. 'Completely spoiled.' Her eyes returned to the bank notes with undisguised fondness.

He had the whole story from her after that; the money worked miracles. She took him into the office to show him the register, and indeed, with some difficulty the year was indeed ascertained as 1806. Beethoven often made mistakes in his dates, and here he had written the sixth of July where he clearly meant the fifth.

And they certified, as well, the presence of a woman, though not, curiously, her identity.

'We had been expecting Beethoven,' Frau Streicher explained. 'We had a reservation in his name. It had come by post the week before. Then she came instead.'

'What was the name?'

'Don't know.'

'Frau Streicher ... Please.'

With genuine perplexity, she said, *I don't know.*

She recalled that the woman was heavily veiled, though not in mourning. With a tired grunt, Frau Streicher brought down the register, blew dust from its cover and opened it. She slowly turned the pages. Finally she found the page she was looking for and jabbed a thick finger at the entry. The woman had signed with an elegant scrawl which was no more legible than a cat's paw.

'Was she married?' Schindler asked, looking down, squinting, trying to decipher the handwriting.

'She was wearing gloves,' said Frau Streicher. And then added irritably, 'What do you expect twenty-one years later? I have a perfectly fine memory, but you expect miracles.'

'Please accept my apologies,' said Schindler, holding his hands up, palms out, in a mollifying gesture.

Indeed, Frau Streicher could not recall a single physical detail about the woman, save that she was neither overly short or especially tall; she was adequately delicate of movement, and somewhat unburdened by luggage.

'I did not pry,' said Frau Streicher clearly and precisely. 'It is against my nature to pry.'

She impressed upon Schindler – with unnatural vehemence, he thought – that, although she did not have a magistrate's mentality, she exercised a certain discretion in such matters as would all decent people. If it were known, or strongly suspected, that assignations of an unhealthy sort might be taking place on her premises she would not countenance it. But this was Beethoven, in any event, famous throughout all of Europe, his name known in every remote hamlet of the Empire. She clearly would exercise extra discretion.

'Beethoven arrived then,' Schindler said.

'The letter came first,' Frau Streicher answered.

Schindler gave a start when he realized that she was pointing at the letter he held in his hand. He gave it to her to examine; straightaway she admitted to having broken the seal herself.

'There was no telling for certain to whom it was addressed,' she explained. 'It had no name, as you can see. But me, I only read the signature and knew that it must go to the lady. And she had not shown her face out of the room. She never came down for dinner; and took only a light meal in her rooms – his rooms, I should say – at midday. I brought the letter up with her tray.'

'You saw her then!' exclaimed Schindler.

'Not exactly,' said Frau Streicher. 'She stood at the window and told me in the coolest way to put the tray down, then thanked me and asked me to leave. I said, "There's a letter for you, Frau—" But she cut me off, so I left it there on the tray.

'Within the hour the woman had packed and gone.' She left no consideration for Frau Streicher, which did not insinuate her into the owner's good graces. Indeed, she had left no trace of herself of any kind. She had stood in front of the hotel with her single bag, pacing to and fro, until the coach came and took her off.

'Beethoven arrived soon after,' said Frau Streicher. 'He was in the best of spirits, though somewhat agitated, which did not strike anyone as out of the ordinary. After all, we had taken care of him before and knew what he was like. A nervous, unpredictable gentleman. He arrived in a state of disorder, but with good will, or so it seemed.

'But once in his room – and I had not had the temerity to warn him, not that it would have done any good – he obviously discovered his lady's absence... There were moments of silence,' Frau Streicher said after a pause to collect her thoughts.

'Moments of silence?' asked Schindler.

'Perhaps you could say the lull before the storm. Before the infernal racket began.'

Once it began, several guests descended to inform Frau Streicher, with considerable agitation, that all might not be well in Room 311. Then from the outside court a coachman entered to note that a heavy chair – or so it seemed from the broken parts scattered in the street – had been hurled out of one of the windows on the second floor. Within moments Frau Streicher mounted the staircase and made her way through the small crowd of affluent, self-made invalids gathered outside the door. Horrible noises came from within. She knocked with strident authority:

'Herr Beethoven! I won't have it! What is the meaning of this? Open up.'

Before she had found the key, surrounded in the candlelight by half a dozen guests in various states of dishabille, the commotion within suddenly ceased. But Beethoven did not come to the door. He made it clear, in various vulgar terms that he wanted to be left alone, although by now that was out of the question. When Frau Streicher unlocked and swung open the door, he was sitting on the bed. A disconsolate figure, though by no means contrite, and he would not meet her gaze nor answer her.

'What have you done to my property?' demanded Frau Streicher repeatedly.

'Your property,' he replied derisively.

She nearly wept at the broken china, and the heavy leaded mirror, smashed to bits on the floor. 'This will have to be paid for. I assure you, Herr Beethoven, someone will have to pay for this.'

Beethoven did not respond. He sat motionless on the bed, staring out the window. It was a fine moonless night with a great bowl of stars as a centrepiece.

'He was clutching it,' recalled Frau Streicher. 'It was crumpled but not torn.' Schindler leaned close to her as her voice had dropped to a whisper. 'In his hand he held the letter which you have brought here today.'

By five o'clock, as twilight darkened to night, Schindler knew he had exhausted Frau Streicher, and learned all she could tell him.

Twenty-one years after the event, in honour of Beethoven's memory and reputation, Schindler, his trusted and devoted factotum, paid for the damage he had caused at the Swan Hotel in Karlsbad in 1806. Schindler had always told Beethoven to be careful with china, and to try to be less clumsy. Even though the great master was dead, Schindler felt compelled to make things right, to clean up the mess.

'Clumsy wasn't the problem,' said Frau Streicher, but she was more than satisfied, the bank notes already locked in a drawer.

'We will leave it at that,' Schindler said with a tight smile. It was to her credit, after all, that she had never pursued him.

'He was a horrible man,' she repeated as Schindler bade her goodbye.

'Good day, Madame,' he replied, and bowed deeply.

Returning to Vienna that evening, Schindler wondered seriously if he should give up this strange quest. Today he had made a beginning; he had carried out a certain task connected to a curiosity found among the effects of the late master. It might be wise, he thought, it might be prudent, to stop here, with this image of a veiled woman in a hotel in Karlsbad. What if a further search, and future disclosures, were to turn out badly and tarnish Beethoven's reputation? What then? Schindler was deeply torn. He wanted to protect the master and yet he felt he could not justify not pursuing the mystery of the Immortal Beloved to its conclusion.

Anton Schindler, more than anything, was a man of conscience. How could he live with himself if he didn't go on?

Chapter 4

The Enchantress

'I must lock the door!'

'But, Countess—'

'We must not be disturbed!'

She hurried past him, turned the key and, with a graceful, balletic movement on her toes, she moved closer to him. With lips that pouted, she said, 'Not *everything* they say about me is true.'

Schindler felt himself blush. He had never become completely accustomed to royalty, and had always kept a polite distance from it, his manner a kind of grave reserve to hide his nervousness. Unlike Beethoven he had never given lessons to the wealthy and had not experienced the sighs and smiles and flirtations that often accompanied music lessons with the daughters of wealthy men. Countess Julia Gallenburg née Guicciardi was seductive, as white and beautiful at forty as a woman could be; or rather, at that age, she maintained at least enough of the seductive charm for which she was reputed, and without touching him, she had the power to make Schindler feel touched. She made herself a place on the divan, and he stood before her feeling somewhat awkward, his hat in his hands.

'Karl Holz was here,' said Julia, 'with that other one, the weasel . . .'

'Johann?' asked Schindler.

'Yes. That one,' said Julia. 'How could Luigi have such a vile brother? It's just shocking that they're related.'

Schindler gave nothing away, but commented, with a touch of irony: 'I trust Holz and Beethoven were in good health.'

'They told me you are attempting to steal Luigi's money,' said the Countess. 'They were positive you would come here.'

'And they were right,' Schindler said.

'But why?'

'It concerns your friendship with Beethoven.'

'I told them nothing,' said Julia. She leaned forward with a glint of complicity in her eyes. 'But the price of my silence is that you must tell me everything.'

'But, no,' said Schindler. 'It falls upon me to interrogate you.'

She tossed her head coquettishly. 'And why should I submit to that?'

Schindler didn't have a good answer to what he imagined was the Countess's unspoken question: what right do *you*, a commoner, have? He said, too stiffly, 'Because it is what Beethoven would have wanted.'

'Then you have to make a promise, Herr Schindler – what I shall tell you will never leave this room.'

'On my word of honour.'

'You want to know about my ... relations with Beethoven?'

'I would like to, yes,' said Schindler earnestly.

The Countess raised her proud head and there was the hint of a smile on her lips, but no irony. She said, 'There is substance to the rumours. More than substance – truth. I was the great love of Luigi's life.'

Was she indeed? Schindler had come to see Countess Gallenburg because he had recalled, on the way back to Vienna, a remark made by Frau Streicher: The Immortal Beloved who waited in Karlsbad was 'like a countess'. Returning to Beethoven's residence, Schindler located in a conversation book from 1823 remarks that struck him as perhaps significant. They were, to tell the truth, quite asinine, and it was altogether embarrassing to think that some of the remarks were his. But he and Beethoven were by then working closely together, and there could be nothing quite so awkward as to be forced to say something clever and intelligent about a subject in which one had no interest.

'Yes,' had said the master, 'I was very much loved by her, far more than her husband ever was.'

They were talking about Countess Guicciardi, and following this pronouncement, Beethoven had added that 'she once came to see me in tears but I spurned her.'

To which Schindler replied, 'Hercules at the cross-roads!' Such a ridiculous comment. More than enough to make one retch, and only some glimmer of posterity prevented Schindler from crossing out the entire conversation. And now, sitting in her drawing room, he realized quite suddenly, that Beethoven had lied to him.

He had been the one head-over-heels in love, not her. Not this flirt of a Countess.

It was clear to Schindler that she was the flirt, that she had doubtless led him on, and he was the Romeo swooning with romantic love. Which was not to say that she had not been attracted to him. Nor that she would not have given herself to him in full or that she was less than sincere. Rather she was the beautiful Julia Guicciardi, who at seventeen could turn any man's head.

'My cousins, Theresa and Josephine Brunswick,' said Countess Julia, 'they knew Beethoven *intimately*.'

'Yes, he spoke of them often,' said Schindler, coughing at an allusion which was unmistakable: Beethoven's piano lessons often came with something extra.

'Beethoven was in his late twenties when we met,' said Julia. 'He was reputed to be noble, sensitive, and cultured.'

And a great virtuoso in a city of fabulous pianists, Schindler wanted to add. The master's playing was not of the old classical sort, but bursting with emotion to such an extent that, when he played in the Viennese salons, men and women were brought to tears, to heaving sobs, such was the power of his performance. Already, by 1800, he had toured Prague, Berlin, and elsewhere in Europe, and played at the court of Frederick Wilhelm.

'I met him at the palace of Count Lichnowsky,' said the Countess, 'where I had gone to hear him for the first time. I was scarcely seventeen. I had heard that his music aroused such passion as to be dangerous. And although he was not so very handsome, I was told he had made conquests which would have made him the envy of many an Adonis.'

Thus she was teased and perhaps aroused by a competitive fervour to captivate him. Excited by the prospect of meeting the young virtuoso, she and her cousins arrived at Count Lichnowsky's palace at 44 Alserstrasse, where Beethoven both lived and worked under the roof of his patron. Julia was ushered into the drawing room after being compelled to wait for the first movement to end – lateness was an incurable habit with her. At the pianoforte she was shocked to see that Beethoven was much handsomer than she had been led to expect: young, physically much more desirable than had been described to her by her jealous cousins – indeed, a man with perfect curls, who played in a state of beautiful and complete concentration. Though not so concentrated that he couldn't cast her a glance in the midst of a smile and a glissando. He was as noble as she had imagined, as refined in spirit as any prince. Overcome by the beauty of the music, she felt literally dizzy. His expression as he looked her way, and the poetry of his hands upon the instrument literally forced her to retire.

'I smile now,' she said to Schindler, her smile rueful. 'I was young.' And once again she became lost in memories.

Recovering her composure in an empty, adjoining salon, Julia sat for a long time watching the flickering candles and listening to the muted sounds of the fabulous music. Her mind was full of his beautiful face, his magic fingers.

Her tumultous thoughts and feelings were suddenly interrupted by harsh laughter. Roused violently from her reverie, she was surprised to see the figure of a man, his back to her, gazing out the window. His loud guffaw was followed by a series of chuckles.

'Oh!' she cried in genuine surprise. 'I didn't see you.'

He cast her a glance, his hands clasped behind his back, a glance loaded with scorn. 'Have you seen a ghost? Why do you look so frightened? Is it the wretched music?'

He came towards her then. He was, in one word, ugly – unshaven, badly dressed, and his face was twisted into a frown which by turns let out sardonic laughter.

'Hello,' he said, and bowed in a peremptory way that ridiculed manners.

She was uneasy, to say the least, and managed to stammer, 'I ... I must go back.'

'You are leaving me, Countess, to listen to that *ass*?'

'The music is beautiful,' she insisted. 'Do you know who that is?'

'An ass who plays like a kitchen maid scrubbing pots, all clipped and staccato.'

'I was told,' said Julia, with the haughtiness of a true countess, 'that the Viennese were possessed of superior taste. Clearly, that's not so in your case.'

He stopped. 'Ah. You must be Julia Guicciardi. I hear there is quite a contest for your charms.'

She was quite taken aback. 'Sir, you are rude and offensive. I am leaving.'

'Tell me,' he said with a taunting smile, 'do you play the piano? It would not surprise me. Do you? Because I intend to be your teacher.'

'What?'

'I shall call on you tomorrow at ten o'clock.' He smiled more broadly, raised his hands and flexed his fingers. 'Be ready!'

He broke out into Homeric laughter which shattered her already fragile composure.

'You will be barred from the house!' she warned with all the imperial wrath a seventeen-year-old countess could muster.

Which did not stop the ugly wretch from turning up next morning as promised, presenting himself in succession to the housekeeper, the butler, the page, and her father, Count Guicciardi. Julia, watching from an upstairs window, was shocked to see the man she had roughly encountered the day before, who was surely a servant, calling at the front door. She fully expected her father to order him away, and box his ears if need be.

Instead, the Count warmly shook the man's hand and invited him inside.

'Fetch Julia!' said her father to the butler, who called to the page, who said to her, 'A gentleman is here to see you.'

She was not at an age where she liked to admit she might be stupid. She fled downstairs, looking for somewhere to hide, and before she reached the bottom step, heard her father crying out above the Homeric laughter, 'He says he is your new piano teacher!'

She decided to confront them. Sternly she said to her father, 'There has been a mistake. This man is a common oaf who accosted me last night in the salon at Prince Lichnowsky's. I insist you send him away at once.'

Her father regarded her with a mixture of perplexity, astonishment and indulgence. 'Julia, I will not send him away. It would be a shame upon our household.'

Still confused, Julia took a step forward, forcing herself to look into the eyes of the ugly, brusque man with no manners. Count Guicciardi put out a hand and said, 'May I present Ludwig van Beethoven.'

He came to give her lessons several times a week. Dressed in an old grey jacket and breeches, his black hair already stringy and wild, he would arrive often with a day's, or even several days', growth of beard. He was mercurial, but at a glance Julia could tell if the lesson would be easy and light-hearted or difficult and stiff, whether Beethoven himself would be charming or preoccupied or – as he was quite often – thoroughly on edge, ready to fly into a rage.

'I insist upon a light touch,' he told her time and time again, and standing over her he would shape her fingers on the keys, so that they were bent and did not lie flat.

'I am sorry,' she said contritely each time, 'but it is the way I was taught.'

'You were taught by fools,' he said. 'Now you are taught by me.'

She did not discourage his attentions. For in spite of his looks – or indeed because of them – she found him seductive, his gaze at times hallucinatory. His personality acted on her like a spell. His hairy fingers covered hers that were so much more delicate; one day as she played, the back of his hand touched the nape of her neck in wordless admiration, and she was thrilled. Julia found herself dreaming of the day that he would simply take her in his arms and she might let down the pretence of her breeding and her station. Why not? Her cousins had toyed with Beethoven before she, and he with them. But her fantasies were more extravagant – and why not? Wasn't she so much more beautiful than her cousins? Blessed with the most delicate features, a small mouth, almond eyes, and dark curls falling across a high forehead, Countess Julia was one of the most sought-after young women in Vienna.

But it was not only the prospect of a heightened sense of romance, played out upon her small mouth and warm white throat, that made Julia's already active fantasy life more vivid. Beethoven's presence in her life affected the way she thought and acted; she took music more seriously, and with it, life itself. She dined one evening at the von Brunswicks, and the guests included her cousins Therese von Brunswick and Josephine with her husband, Count Deym – thirty years her senior, a military man in bearing, and a monarchist and a philistine by conviction. The dapper young Count Gallenburg – whom she had earlier mistaken for Beethoven – was there as well, seated next to her, still physically charming if not so intelligent and talented as she had once supposed. He turned to her and said innocently, 'You must attend my next recital.'

'Yes, I shall. I heard you that Sunday—'

'Oh! I know!'

'The music was beautiful.'

But Count Gallenburg, who sensed the insincerity in her remark, frowned. Before taking lessons with Beethoven, Julia would indeed have found the Count's playing just as beautiful as she found the man himself physically, but her appreciation of fine music, if not her talent, had grown immensely under Beethoven's tutelage. It was no longer possible for her to lie convincingly about music; through Beethoven it had become too important to her.

Beside her the coquettish Josephine, feeling more than a touch of rivalry now that she was married,

41

exclaimed, 'Surely the Count's playing can't be *that* bad! You are such a hopeless liar, Julia.'

Count Gallenburg shrugged, attempted a smile, and looked miserable.

Across from Julia, the dour and aging Count Deym wiped his wooden teeth with his napkin and nodded in his wife's direction. 'Personally I found Count Gallenburg's playing exquisite. It's that damn Beethoven I can't stand. People only claim to admire his stuff so as not to seem ignorant.'

'But my dear husband,' said Josephine, 'don't parade your stupidity in front of our guests. Julia, we can all speak frankly here. Tell us your opinion of Count Gallenburg's playing, if you please?' Her smile was wicked, challenging.

'Heavens, no!' broke in the young Count, maintaining his forced grin with effort. 'I was not looking for flattery.'

'Too clipped and staccato,' replied Julia immediately. 'Not enough singing tone.' She smiled at him and touched his sleeve. 'Sorry.'

Count Gallenburg, expecting to field a compliment, froze his expression in a half-smile; Count Deym grunted disapproval. Julia's father intervened, saying, 'My daughter, as you can see, is taking lessons from the maestro himself.'

'What?' exclaimed Josephine.

'Beethoven comes every day to the house,' said the Count.

'He takes no money,' Julia hastened to add. 'But he will accept some linen if I can persuade him that I sewed it myself.'

'Then you do sew,' quipped Count Gallenburg.

Julia felt her cousin bristle with jealousy, as though she herself had not been subject to the stress and strain Beethoven put upon the bodice. 'Do you think it wise?' asked Josephine.

'What do you mean?' asked her husband sharply.

'I mean, he is a harsh teacher,' said Josephine quickly.

'He is a scoundrel and a republican,' said Count Deym. 'I have even heard it said that he is a follower of Napoleon. Make no mistake. He'd have us all in the arms of Madame Guillotine! He travels in polite society on his reputation as a virtuoso, but flies into a fit, so I understand, if anyone dare suggest he sit down before a keyboard and himself play. What conceit! He has been known to say, "There have been thousands of princes. There is only one Beethoven!"'

'Did you ever hear him play?' asked Josephine; and Julia, glancing her way, saw her eyes drop with a guilty secret.

'No,' admitted Julia. 'Not yet.'

'Who has?' demanded the Count. 'He came to Vienna ten years ago, and played his way to success but now rests on his laurels.'

'I heard him play,' said Therese, who until now had remained silent. 'And it was something you had to witness. It was difficult to believe that it was the same instrument we all hear bashed and thumped by others.'

Julia was perplexed. 'I wonder why he will no longer play?'

'Beethoven,' said his young colleague, Count Gallenburg, 'is a strange and obstinate man. He says that to be compelled to play makes him feel like a servant, and that he serves no master.'

'But,' said Count Deym pointedly, glancing at Julia, 'he does take a bit of linen, doesn't he?'

The entire table, save Julia, broke into laughter.

As Julia continued her lessons with Beethoven, she grew confused by his extremes of attention and indifference. There were days he would be all patience and concern, and stay at the house four or five hours, now serious, now playful. But there were sessions, and long ones, when he was alone in a world of his own, intensely contemplative and frightening in the quality of his remoteness. One day, playing Bach inventions while Ludwig sat at the table staring into space as though in deep reflection, Julia was seized by a whim. She made a mistake, and when he did not react, she felt annoyed. Deliberately she made another. Then she distorted a whole passage. Finally she stopped playing entirely and cried, 'Luigi!'

Banging shut the lid finally drew his attention. Startled, he turned to her.

'I made a mistake,' she said contritely.

'You think that because I did not stop you that I was not listening? One mistake is nothing. But the fact that you thump out the notes without the least sensitivity to their meaning is inexcusable. Your lack of passion is unforgivable. Your...

'I...'

He smiled at her horrified expression. 'I shall have to beat you.'

She was relieved that he was not angry and replied coyly, 'I hear that you pinch some of your students.'

'And others I bite on the neck.'

She put forth her hand, only to have him slap it

harder than she anticipated. She recoiled. Then, as he approached the keyboard, she got up, making room for him. Would he play? He studied the keyboard. Was he now, for the first time, going to play for her?

Nothing of the sort. He crashed both hands on the keyboard like a mischievous child. And roared with laughter.

It was as though a coiled demon lived within him, ready to strike. Those afternoons when her lessons ended early, Beethoven sometimes invited her to take a walk with him through Vienna and she always accepted. He walked every day, for at least two hours, and when they were not talking he was humming to himself. He always carried a sketchbook, and if a musical idea occurred to him, he would jot it down immediately.

One day they took a promenade in the Schonbrunn Gardens behind the Hapsburg Palace. It was one of Julia's favourite places, with its grand terraces and beautiful Neptune fountain, where she had played as a child the first time she visited Vienna. Here Beethoven turned to her and said, 'I am writing a new symphony.'

They were walking towards a group of dukes and duchesses, some of whom she knew, and Beethoven was striding forwards a little too fast, and she felt him squeeze her arm.

'It will cause a scandal,' said Beethoven. 'Because of its subject.'

'Tell me!'

'Take my arm.'

Suddenly they barged together through the cluster of royalty, impolitely forcing them to stand aside. Shocked words and insults followed them.

'Luigi!' she cried. 'How could you?'

'They must make their way for us, not we for them,' Beethoven said. 'Their days are over. Their world is finished. When I was a boy, they'd have had you arrested for less. But now they are scared of what happened in France.' He laughed. 'Do you know why wigs have gone out of fashion? Too many ended up in the bottom of baskets!'

'But I am a countess, Luigi.'

'They are frightened – of Napoleon,' said Beethoven.

Napoleon of France, then first consul, having usurped the Directory and preserved the gains of the French revolution, threatened to bring an end to the feudal order wherever it persisted in Europe. He planned to put in its place a system of laws and republican government.

'And that is why I intend to dedicate my symphony to Napoleon Bonaparte.'

Of all this Julia understood perhaps not quite half. But the history, the politics that so absorbed Beethoven meant little to her; the essential thing – essential by her standards – came soon after. One afternoon Beethoven came to her, and instead of a lesson they took a ride in a carriage. His heroic symphony, on which he had been composing all day, had left him in an aroused and stimulated state. She may have been a countess, she may have been a virgin, but on that afternoon none of it mattered. He stared at her a long while before taking her face in his hands. Staring deeply into her eyes he suddenly began to kiss her. She felt a surge of abandon that drowned any reticence as his rough skin rubbed against her cheeks and lips, as his lips found hers with warm and demanding kisses. When he lifted her dress – the carriage clattering along all the while – she did not resist. She married her lips to his and clung to him while he took her, not brutally but with great feeling, as she cried out again and again.

Chapter 5

A Sonata

People did not easily talk to Anton Schindler about being in love. They found him too stiff, too like a schoolmaster in his comportment, which was indeed becoming more rigid with the passing years. On the other hand, he was aware of this and so he made efforts to compensate, to use his lawyerly instincts and not to be hasty in judgement. It was not easy for him; but to Countess Gallenburg, who had been in love as many times as there are turtle doves beneath the eves in Vienna, his natural censoriousness perhaps made little difference. He hoped so.

He said, 'The Master was composing the Eroica, then.' And added, smiling, 'Bursting through a phalanx of dukes and duchesses.'

'Yes,' said the countess. 'And he was in love with me.'

Schindler nodded. Even now there were vestiges of the Countess's youthful beauty; he could well imagine Beethoven's infatuation, if not love for this woman. He said quickly, 'Who would not in those years have been in love with the Countess?'

It was obviously the wrong thing to say. *In those years*. What a fool you are, Schindler, he thought. As soon as the words left his lips he wanted to retrieve them.

She regarded him strangely, as if he were some kind of exotic bird. 'He wanted to marry me.'

'Yes, he always spoke highly of you,' Schindler lied. He added, 'Even long after.'

'For my part it seems like yesterday,' said the countess, her eyes soft with a looking-inward quality.

'You were always in his thoughts, I'm sure,' said Schindler, attempting to atone for his earlier lack of tact.

And at that the countess laid her finely coiffed head back on the divan and laughed in a derisive, throaty, though not unfriendly, way. 'He was in love with me,' she said again, and in a tone that left no space for debate or question.

And it was true: Beethoven had been in love with her. He had written: There have been some moments of complete bliss, and this is the first time I have ever felt that marriage could make me happy.

And the fact was, Schindler now learned, he had sent a proposal to Julia's father, Count Guicciardi. That Beethoven was thirty and his intended scarcely twenty was surely not of grave significance. That he had come from Bonn with a van attached to his name suggested royalty and did not make it an impossible match – unless someone happened to look into it, because the Beethoven line from which Ludwig was descended was no more noble than your average blacksmith. But it was a rather unlikely match, given that Beethoven was – the far greater sin – not rich. This occurred to the count immediately.

Was Countess Julia in love with Beethoven? She was indeed, and deeply, emphatically so. She woke in the morning, and her first thoughts were of Beethoven. She found him in her mind constantly during her morning ablutions, which was in her experience a sure sign of love. She liked to sew, and spent part of every morning making things for Beethoven of linen and wool. At her drawing lesson, if she had a moment to sketch freely, she invariably found herself pencilling his wild hair. Then there were the lessons with him in the afternoon, which could be intense in the feelings they elicited and left her exhausted by evening when, over supper, she was preoccupied with her beloved. Julia was indeed in love; Beethoven was never out of her thoughts for more than a few moments during the course of a day. The fact that she was frequently seeing, at the same time, Count Gallenburg, took nothing away from the profundity of her great love for Beethoven.

Some would find the scene that followed amusing; it was at any rate ironic, even touching.

'Julia, I have a proposal of marriage,' said her father, summoning her to his study one day. 'From a composer.'

Julia felt her heart jump – she had known it was coming, and still ... Could the great master actually be proposing to her? It was a dream, a sweet, impossible dream. She felt faint and giddy with anticipation.

But then her world came crashing down around

her when her father said, 'Count Wenzel Robert von Gallenburg has asked for your hand in marriage.'

She could not believe it. She *refused* to believe it.

'I have talked to the count myself, and his intentions are honourable.'

Tears welled in her eyes, but not for joy. She liked Count Gallenburg, but this was not the same as love. This had nothing to do with love.

Her father saw she was upset and confused, and he said, 'You are not thinking of Beethoven, are you?'

She nodded, wordlessly, trying to hold back a flood of tears.

'I have his proposal as well.'

Julia's heart leaped. Still rarer than one marriage proposal was two – and the second one meant everything to her. Beethoven *did* love her.

The count sighed heavily, and pointed to a fairly illegible letter on his desk. 'Julia, the gossip is everywhere.'

'But there is no contest, Papa!' cried Julia. 'Not between the two of them.' She leapt up and spontaneously embraced the old count. She realized that at that moment she felt as happy as she had ever felt in her life.

'You love Beethoven?'

She nodded vigorously, blushing deeply with both joy and shyness.

Her father shook his head. 'No, my dear, I'm sorry. I cannot give my consent. It's impossible.'

'But, Papa—'

'We are not wealthy, Julia. If Beethoven had some money ... but even then such a match would seem entirely unsuitable. The fact is, he is a man without rank, fortune or permanent engagement. And his character and temperament are so peculiar that I doubt anyone, and most surely you, my dear, could find happiness with him.'

'He is a genius,' cried Julia.

'That may be. But in the last year he has not played or published a single note. He is supposed to be a great virtuoso. Indeed, I have heard him and can attest to it. But he no longer plays, as much as his improvisations were marvellous, and isn't one definition of a virtuoso that he produce? Some say it is because of his Napoleonism. He is too busy with politics. But there are others who say there is some infirmity that prevents him.'

'Untrue gossip from evil tittle tattlers!' said Julia. 'People are always quick to bring greatness down to their size.'

The count regarded her with a mixture of fondness and sadness. He loved his impetuous daughter, so quick to follow the dictates of her heart, and he found it difficult to deny her anything. But the last thing he wanted was to see her hurt, and he was certain that Beethoven, as a husband, would give her nothing but misery. 'Has he ever played for you?' he asked.

'No,' she had to admit. By now there had been months of lessons, and however ardently she pressed him, he refused to play for her, and she had begun to wonder herself. Yet she spoke up for him, saying, 'You know that envy and criticism follow him everywhere.'

'I only know,' said the count, 'that it is not a proper match for you.'

Although Julia could not change her father's mind — even with a grand show of tears that usually weakened his resolve – she knew him as a man who recognized a good bargain. And for the fading coin of nobility, there were bargains to be made. If Count Gallenburg, because of his wealth and desirable lineage, could be a good match in spite of being a poor musician, why not Ludwig van Beethoven, a genius who had publishers banging on his door morning till night? A man who was beloved of emperors and kings, and had entrée to courts throughout Europe? Also, she pointed out in her impassioned plea make Beethoven's case, it might be that the van in his name was Dutch nobility. In the end Julia and the count struck a deal.

'Prove to me that your Beethoven can still play, and I will give my consent, and you may marry whom you wish.'

Count Guicciardi found himself in a state of conflict. On the one hand, he was certain that Beethoven was an altogether inappropriate husband for his daughter – an older man with strange ways and a background certain to be undesireable. And, worst of all, the man was impoverished. But, at the same time, the count had a serious interest in music and was thrilled by his proximity to such undeniable genius. The wager with his daughter came on the heels of the arrival in their house of one of the new pianos built by John Broadwood in England; the count had been encouraged to purchase it by Beethoven himself. And the crucial question for the count was this: would the master – indeed *could* the master – play? The count was betting his daughter's hand that he could not. And so it was that Julia wrote to Beethoven.

Beloved Luigi,

My father has recently taken delivery of a new pianoforte, from John Broodwood & Co. in London. It produces five octaves and we think it is the first of its kind in Vienna. If you would like to test it yourself, you are of course welcome. The tuner shall come tomorrow, and on Sunday I shall not be able to have my lesson as we are going to the country. But if you should wish to come in the afternoon, between one and six, you will find yourself quite alone, and I would welcome it if you would inaugurate this fine instrument yourself and describe to me your frank impressions of it.

When Beethoven arrived – he was not about to let such an opportunity be wasted – the house was indeed empty, and he found the new piano proudly occupying the music room. He opened the lid and examined the piano carefully, pleased by its iron frame and sound-board of pure spruce. He sat down and was satisfied with the sonority and repetition capabilities of the keys, hammering on several, dozens of times.

Julia knew all this not because Beethoven told her afterwards, but because she was there as a hidden witness. She and her father watched Beethoven from a passageway concealed in the music room. They had not gone to the country; that was merely a ruse. Rather, they stood sharing a single peephole.

'I don't think he will play,' whispered her father after several moments had passed. 'I told you.'

'He is just examining it, Papa. Wait.'

'I doubt that he will play at all.'

Julia put her eye to the peephole. Beethoven was now

sitting at the piano and staring in front of him. After what seemed to be a great length of time, during which he did not stir, he crashed down his hands on the keyboard and produced a C-sharp chord – with a miss. The chord was ugly and resonated in the music room unpleasantly. He played the chord again, with the same result. It was disturbing.

'Julia...'

She knocked her father's hand off her shoulder as she watched in dismay. Slowly Beethoven leaned his head forward until at last his right ear rested against the soundboard. He tried the chord again – successfully this time – and sustained the music with the pedal.

'At least he can play a chord,' said Julia's father. 'That *is* a chord.'

With his head still lying on the piano, Beethoven began to play arpeggios in C-sharp minor. They became a blur of sound, he played so quietly. She turned away, unable to watch and be further disappointed. She avoided her father's gaze.

'I told you,' he said. 'Something is amiss. Something is very, very wrong.'

But no sooner had she stopped watching than the unremarkable noise she had been listening to was transformed into something else. A slow – not mournful, yet dark – adagio reached her ears. After a few bars, it suddenly sent a flash of heat through her entire body. What he was playing, his head lowered to within an inch of the keys, sounded like a sonata, and she stood transfixed to the spot. Slowly she turned to her father, who was struck dumb as well. She had never heard a thing of such beauty. The music flooded her interior, flooded her with an aching warmth, all the more because there was no theme repeated, simply the almost baroque unravelling of something different from anything she had ever heard before.

'My god!' exclaimed the count. 'Beethoven!' He shook his head in wonderment. 'The music is sublime!'

Julia left the passageway, entranced. The appeal of the music was liberating, and she could not bear hiding from it and from its composer, the man she loved. The music stirred her deeply, which was not something that she was used to. As she moved towards the music room and quietly opened the door, she had the sense of being within his space, his personal space, delimited by the music that came not only from his hands but his soul. He was in a deep reverie, his eyes closed. There was something childlike about him, something that removed years from his face, as he concentrated on the tones he produced; and perhaps that was why she gave way to such great stupidity.

She called out lightly, 'Luigi . . .'

At first he did not hear her but continued to play. Even then, given a second chance, she did not perceive the profanity of entering into, and perhaps fracturing, his rapture. As inspired as he was at that moment, and deeply at one with his own music, her intrusion was not what he needed or wanted. Certainly not at that moment. Nonetheless, she softly reached out to run fingers through his locks in the same way she had done so many times before – seriously and yet playfully.

The piano crashed into silence. Beethoven jumped up as though scalded, violently kicking the piano stool backwards. The sudden force of his rage struck her almost like a physical blow.

'What is the meaning of this?'

'Luigi ... I—'

'You have played a trick on me!' He caught a glimpse across her shoulder of Count Guicciardi who stood hesitantly in the doorway.

'No one was to be here. *No one!*'

'But we wanted to hear you play, Luigi,' she said, her voice trembling. 'We meant no harm. We only wanted to hear you play. And you were playing so very, very beautifully ...' She began to weep, which only made him angrier still.

'I have been tricked! Treated like a ... trained dog! Like some object that belongs to you. But I belong to no one, don't you understand that? *No one!*'

Count Guicciardi rushed forward, at once confused and yet relieved – he realized that any concerns he had about marriage between his daughter and this madman were over. He grasped Julia by the shoulders to comfort her while at the same time expostulating, 'Herr Beethoven! I beg you, calm down! You are among friends!'

'Ah! Now I see. Friends!' He spit out the words.

'We mean you no harm. The music ... it was—'

'Not for you to hear.' Beethoven slammed down the piano lid. 'I see perfectly. It's all so clear, isn't it? A test of my abilities. An exhibition for sceptics. Spying through the peephole upon servants at the keyboard!' He glared at them. 'Who am I? Am I Beethoven, composer?'

Julia put her hands together, supplicating. 'Please, Luigi, I can't stand to—'

'Am I Beethoven, virtuoso?'

She wanted to plead with him, to break through his withering sarcasm; her mouth was open but no words came forth. She was chocked with fear and confusion.

'Or Beethoven, the misanthrope! The madman! The eccentric!'

He did not wait for an answer. He stormed out of the music room and down the grand staircase, with Julia chasing after him.

He turned once, and said to her in full fury, 'What you have done is terrible. You have robbed me of my most treasured feelings. I swear by everything I hold sacred that you will never see me again.'

He fled the house, and Julia ran after him, shouting, 'Father can go to hell! Really, Luigi, I mean it. I love you! I swear I will be your wife! Please, Luigi, listen to me. Don't leave me now. I swear on all that's holy ... I love you. Please don't leave me. *Please*...'

But he never turned back. And when her father reached her, taking hold of her, she heard him say, 'It's no use, Julia. He cannot hear you. So much is clear now. His head resting on the keys as he played. Don't you see? The poor man is deaf, or close to it.'

Within a month, the beautiful Countess Guicciardi – the 'enchantress', as she was known in society circles – married the young and handsome Count von Gallenburg. It was a beautiful wedding in the best Viennese tradition, and as a marriage it was a thorough disaster, soon leading, on her part, to boredom and numerous lovers. If the countess was not capable of feeling things as deeply as Beethoven, she felt them many depths more profoundly than the shallow young nobleman who was content to scrape along as an uninspired musical director for the rest of his life. That Count Gallenburg was an ignorant fool was something to which Schindler himself could attest; he had exchanged some severe words with the composer over the merits, in fact, of Beethoven.

Now, more than a quarter century later, sunlight and shadow in late afternoon played across the fine piano in the rooms of the Countess Gallenburg née Guicciardi. The countess was tired, and both regret and sadness showed in her eyes. It was a brave act, thought Schindler, for her to have told him so much with no attempt at gloss or self-protection. He fidgeted now, uncomfortable in his role eliciting love affairs out of the past. He asked, 'So you never heard from him again?'

'He wrote to me years later,' said the countess. 'During the siege of the city and Napoleon's invasion, we had some unpleasantness, the count and I. Beethoven wrote to me.'

'But your love affair with Ludwig, once ended, was never reignited?'

The countess did not reply.

He regarded her gently. 'Would you tell me ... if it were?'

She smiled, just faintly, regarding him; he withdrew his gaze. 'If it were...?' she said.

'Would you tell me, for example, if you set a rendez-vous with Beethoven at Karlsbad in 1806? Whether failed or not? Would you tell me that, Countess Gallenburg?'

He realized that he was on dangerous ground baldly asking after the morals of a married woman with four children and, though with no fine reputation for fidelity, a good Catholic. But she was Viennese, and ought to have understood. The countess smiled, rose and went to a small bureau. Unlocking a drawer, she removed a score.

'He sent me this,' she said.

It was a fair copy of the score for the sonata in C-sharp minor that Beethoven had played that day when all went wrong between them. *The Moonlight Sonata*, as critic Hoffman had described and named it.

'"Sonata quasi una fantasia",' said the countess. '"Dedicated to the Countess Julia Guicciardi." I was very touched. But the publishers never printed it that way.'

Schindler took the manuscript and examined it. He looked up at the countess and said, 'I promise you that the next edition will bear your dedication.'

Schindler left soon after, at dusk, and not until he was safely in his carriage did he ask himself: was Countess Gallenburg the Immortal Beloved? Could it have been she? He was certain that he knew the answer but he told himself it was too early to make absolutely certain. He had to continue on his quest.

The countess had reminded Schindler of something important about Beethoven; it was contained in the testament that his brother Johann was trying to pass off as a will. For although the master's hearing still functioned in those days, however poorly, already it was beginning to fail and to isolate him from others; and Beethoven had written: *They who think me hostile, obstinate or misanthropic, how unjust they are to me, for they do not know the secret reason I appear that way*.

Indeed, Schindler could still see Beethoven – a much older Beethoven – walking through Vienna, head down, hands behind his back, so concentrated in thought and absorbed in silence.

It is not possible for me to say: speak louder, shout, I

am deaf. How can I live if my enemies, who are many, believe I no longer possess the one sense that should be perfect to a higher degree in me than in others?

And so that afternoon it was brought home to Anton Schindler – and he silently thanked the countess as she deigned to let him kiss her hand – that Ludwig van Beethoven was not merely a god among men. He was not merely the greatest composer who had ever walked the earth. No: he was, by the very fact of his deafness, so much more vulnerable a man than most – and yet fated, it seemed, to lose the thing he loved. The woman he loved. The Immortal Beloved.

Chapter 6

Three Brothers Beethoven

If Countess Guicciardi *were* the Immortal Beloved, it would be entirely of a piece – it would fit *perfectly* – with Beethoven's lifelong fascination with aristocratic and high-born women. Noble and unattainable, but also women with the leisure and means to practise the piano and develop the taste and delicacy of expression that would elicit the feelings which Beethoven called love.

Schindler was familiar with the names of several of Beethoven's aristocratic and high-born women: Julie von Vering ('with all the virtues of gentle womanliness, the noblest of feelings for nature and art', so her tombstone read, for she died in 1809), who finally married one of Beethoven's good friends; Bettina Brentano, friend of Goethe and wife of the poet von Arnim; the beautiful Antonie Brentano, her sister-in-law, unhappy spouse and surely Beethoven's loyal friend; not to mention the von

Brunswick sisters, or Baroness Ertmann or Princess Odescalchi.

Indeed, it would make Anton Schindler, and perhaps the whole world, happy to discover that the Immortal Beloved was a woman of noble birth. But Beethoven's attraction to women was by no means limited to the high born. This was a truth Schindler already knew, and it came home to him with great force, in fact, when a few days later he again was brought face to face with brother Johann and Karl Holz.

Schindler had gone by mailcoach to the unpleasant mining village of Iglau to see Karl, Beethoven's nephew, who for several months, following his failed suicide attempt, had been enlisted as a cadet in the regiment of Field Marshal von Stutterheim. Schindler intended on making a courtesy visit, nothing else; important because Karl, although he had hurried to Vienna, had missed his uncle's funeral. But when Schindler arrived at the regimental headquarters, he was turned away. He was made to wait at the gate outside the barracks, prevented from entering by the sentry. It rained steadily as he waited and he worried about catching pneumonia. After two hours not Karl but Stutterheim's adjutant came out to see him. The officer was eminently Prussian, scarcely civil, and in a high, stern voice said officiously, 'Your request to visit Officer Cadet Karl van Beethoven has been denied.'

Schindler was furious. 'This is preposterous! I have urgent business concerning his uncle's estate. You can't possibly prevent me from—'

'I have instructions to ensure your safe escort off the premises.'

'Whose decision is this? I demand to see this young man.'

The adjutant smiled acidly. 'You may be escorted at gunpoint if necessary.'

On the parade ground a troop of lancers were exercising, and Schindler spotted Karl among them. In fact, he made out the very pair of boots which he himself had packed and sent off scarcely three months before. He shouted after the young man, which only drew a blank, bloodless glance from Karl, and a threatening gesture on the part of the adjutant, who cried, 'Be gone, Herr Schindler!'

Bitterly disappointed, Schindler turned away. He had come out of civility, not love, and this rejection reignited his anger. It was Beethoven who had loved his nephew, not he; in fact Schindler often felt in the grip of an unwonted rage against the twenty-one-year-old Karl and often enumerated in his mind the boy's offences against the master. Schindler had suppressed these feelings of hostility to come to Iglau, and what had he received for his efforts? A fine Prussian greeting: a kick in the behind.

All this he could have swallowed but then, just as he was climbing into his coach for the return ride to Vienna – wet and lacerated by severe pangs of lumbago at the prospect of a back-wrenching return journey; in short, entirely enervated – he saw a hired carriage bearing down on him. It stopped abreast. Inside it carried none other than Karl Holz and Johann Beethoven. The lanky Holz swung open the door, jumped out and was ready with a smile.

'Herr Schindler,' he cried. 'Tell me: have you not yet found the Immortal Beloved?'

Schindler did not return his smile. 'Have *you*?' he asked.

Johann alighted as well, and said with an overbearing note of triumph, 'They didn't let you see Karl, did they?'

Holz nodded at the old pharmacist. 'I would say that our journey was unnecessary, Herr Beethoven.'

Schindler felt persecuted; why was he going to all this trouble when everyone seemed to be against him? He was ready to abandon the whole business, the search for the Immortal Beloved, and it was only his fidelity to the master's memory that prevented him. A sense of intolerable frustration and indignation coursed through him. 'Why have you kept me from speaking to Karl?'

'We have done nothing of the kind,' said Johann with heavy sarcasm. 'Although, to tell the truth, we were going to try. We hoped to make him sturdy in his resolve. As you can see, we were too late, but no matter. Karl made a wise decision and he made it of his own volition. And I know why – he has no wish to speak of his uncle, my brother, ever again. And he wants nothing that belongs to him. Hardly a surprise, given the circumstances, I should say. Wouldn't you agree, Herr Schindler?'

Schindler stared, holding back his rage. At that moment he hated all the Beethovens without reservation. All those who had been born, those who were dead, and those who still lived. They ought to have remained beet farmers in Antwerp, and to hell with them. He turned on his heel and climbed back into his own carriage. He heard Holz and Johann behind him.

'Where are you going? Not so fast!' cried Johann. He

produced and unfolded a letter. 'Read this, why don't you? A missive from the great composer. Found amongst the letters of a good pharmacist of Linz.'

'I didn't know there was a good pharmacist in Linz,' joked Holz.

'Read this,' repeated Johann, thrusting the letter at Schindler.

It was a letter from Beethoven to Johann, and as he made out the scrawl, Schindler felt break against him in full force a wave of injustice and humiliation, which he had experienced often enough when the master was alive. His eyes flew along the text until he saw the passage they wanted to him to read:

Dear Brother
I avoid that mean and contemptible fellow Schindler
as much as possible ... He is however sometimes
useful, even though he never fails to annoy me with
his ignorance.

Johann snatched back the letter. He laughed. 'Still looking for the woman? Like the French say: *Cherchez la femme?*'

'I think,' said Holz, 'that Herr Schindler's foolishness has got the best of him.'

'His foolishness,' said Johann, 'is hoisting him on his own petard. After my brother's death, just as before.'

'That letter must sit well,' returned Schindler, 'in the head of a man whose brother could not stand to pronounce his name.' He prepared to climb into the coach again, and shot a glance back. 'Goodbye, pseudo-brother.'

Holz, restraining Johann from attacking Schindler, said, 'Come along now. Don't bother with the poor, pathetic man.'

'No,' said Johann angrily. He pulled at Schindler's shoulder, turning him around, dropped his pince-nez and put his face close. 'Let me tell you something, Schindler—'

'If you refuse to help me,' said Schindler, 'I have nothing further to say and need listen to no more from you.'

'I can help you all right,' replied Johann testily. 'I can tell you this much, Herr Immortal Beloved. You'll find no lady at the end of your search. My brother hated women. Hated the sight and smell of them. Make no mistake. That is all you need to know.'

It was such a stupid and crass thing to say, Schindler thought, and yet he recognized, though scarcely consciously, that in his foolish way Johann was trying to tell him something – perhaps of substance and not simply from the stupidity of spleen. In a tone suddenly reasonable and almost gentle, Schindler said, 'Tell me why you said that.'

'What? What do you mean?' Johann retreated a step, suddenly confused, taken aback by Schindler's interest.

'Explain to me why you said that.'

Johann regarded him with a look of surprise. 'You mean about women?'

'If you please,' said Schindler.

'Let's be off,' said Holz, taking Johann's arm.

'Don't be an ass,' said Schindler. 'Here is my carriage. Let yours go.'

'We came by stage,' said Holz.

'Precisely,' said Schindler. He turned to Johann and

said, 'Let us go into town. Even this fool, Holz, can come, too. We'll return to Vienna by the same coach tonight. Meanwhile, we can stop down in a beer house, and you can tell me what you mean about your brother and women.'

The relationship between Beethoven and his brothers was a mystery to all Vienna. That a great composer might be saddled with wretched, non-achieving relatives was not a surprise; it was rather that he would remain close to them, and sometimes, indeed, sink to their level of baseness. But its roots were in Bonn, long ago, and although the Master seldom discussed his first decade of life, Schindler knew the basic facts: there were three of them – Beethoven the eldest, then Caspar and Johann, the baby. Their mother, Maria Magdalene, died in 1789 when Ludwig was seventeen. His father, a music teacher and court tenor to the Elector at Bonn, combined the gentle features of a jovial burgher with a drunk's explosive temper. Rarely sober as he grew older, ready with a switch at the slightest provocation, he was impossible to live with, and was finally a shame on the family.

But Johann van Beethoven had high hopes for his firstborn son, whose talents were evident by the age of four. He hoped to make of him a prodigy, and as soon as the boy's fingers could play notes on the clavier, he drilled him mercilessly. Coming home drunk at night with his friends, he would wake young Ludwig and force him to play until dawn. If Ludwig played poorly, he was shut away in the cellar. Johann van Beethoven exhibited his son to paying listeners, and then finally in Cologne, in 1778, he attempted to present Ludwig as a new Mozart. That proved to be a disaster, perhaps because the elder Beethoven had stifled all the child's attempts at improvisation.

'Our father died in 1792, soon after Ludwig left Bonn,' Johann told Schindler. 'We followed our brother to Vienna – Caspar and I. First Caspar, then I followed him a few years later, after I finished my apothecary's apprenticeship. Ludwig had charge of our estate, and so it was best to be near him. And he wanted us.' After hesitating, Johann added, 'We were still truly brothers in those days...'

In Vienna, Caspar, who could play the piano, taught music to students whom his brother Ludwig sent him. A squat, red-haired runt of a man, Caspar had none of Beethoven's innate genius or acquired manners, feeling or taste. It was not surprising that he tired of giving lessons; he soon began working as a petty functionary in the state bank, which gave him time to help Ludwig, who could not multiply or even do the simplest sums. In his tasks as secretary and business manager, there was more than considerable room to take advantage of Beethoven's growing stature. There were opportunities to sell and resell his famous brother's works, taking off something extra for himself rather generously from the sales. Caspar was no slouch when it came to taking financial advantage, although his crude nature and sanctimonious hypocrisy alienated the polite and refined business world of music.

'But that was Caspar,' Schindler said to Johann, encouraging him to talk. '*You* were honest.'

'That is saying a good deal,' said Holz, laughing.

The three of them sat – like brothers themselves, Schindler thought wryly – in a lowly, dark beer house in Iglau, waiting for the stagecoach back to Vienna.

'Caspar had his reasons,' said Johann, shaking his head. He skimmed the foam off a glass of beer with his mouth. 'May I tell you frankly, or is it clear to you by now? Ludwig treated us piggishly. Not at first, but later.'

'I don't see any point in desecrating the master's memory,' said Schindler defensively. 'No useful purpose is served.' It was always like this with Johann, this constant railing at the master. 'Brothers often behave badly with each other.'

All three, when it came down to it, acted in unseemly ways. They argued and fought often, and their altercations were followed by renewed vows of love and wreaths of kisses and embraces. The effusive extremes of affection and hostility were ever present among the emotionally unstable Beethoven boys.

'Yet what I say is true,' insisted Johann. 'You know how he treated his nephew, and you certainly know how he could maltreat those close to him – even such as you.'

'In some cases, we would say the treatment was deserved,' said Holz.

'All right,' admitted Schindler, ignoring Holz, 'we all know that much of Beethoven. And now you say—'

'I say there was nothing more horrible,' said Johann, leaning forward, speaking in a confidential whisper, 'than the way he dealt with Caspar and me when it came to *women*.'

The anecdote Johann related dated back about twenty years, to an era that was of particularly keen interest to Schindler at the moment. 'It was about 1805 or 1806,' mused Johann. All three brothers spent the summer in Baden, that prosperous and newly designated electorate with its ancient mineral springs – and, Schindler quickly reckoned in his mind, it was not long after Ludwig had broken off with Countess Julia Guicciardi. Sometime during that summer Caspar fell in love with a young woman in town.

'It was not lust,' said Johann, 'or perhaps it was, but Caspar was smitten, that's certain. And Ludwig may have been nursing wounds inflicted by this or that young countess, but I can tell you he was not taken up with melancholy yearnings.'

One afternoon after a session in a beer house, Caspar took Ludwig and Johann to meet his new love, about whom he enthused, though they still scarcely knew one another. Ludwig was reluctant to go, Caspar insisted. They staggered through the disorderly streets of the old commercial district of the city half drunk. The sight of the three of them, like rebel soldiers in search of a bordello, caused onlookers to point at them and titter. Accosting goats, kicking chickens out of their path, embracing fenceposts, they meandered along. Caspar, led the way, silencing his boisterous brothers as they followed him down a back alley to an upholsterer's shop.

'Brothers,' he told them, with a wide, drunken grin, 'let me show you the most beautiful creature in the Empire.'

In the courtyard, as they peered through slats and over the gate, a young woman came into view. Clad in a simple work dress, her hair covered, she carried a heavy roll of fabric in a strangely masculine way – though she possessed, upon even the most cursory inspection, an attractive bust and good broad hips. In fact, Beethoven was quick to point out to Caspar, a *fine* bust and an *excellent* set of hips. She put down the fabric, measured and cut the cloth with expertise and grace. She was beguiling; Caspar had not misled his brothers.

'She was agreeable to look at,' Johann told Schindler who sat hunched over his mug of beer, listening intently. 'Any man would have been taken with her.'

'Yes, yes, go on,' said Schindler. It was painful for him to hear about the master in such a demeaning situation.

Johann continued. Looking up from her work Johanna glimpsed the three brothers watching her. She smiled and cocked her head, not with modesty but with a secure sense of her own physical virtues, and she continued her work, knowing she was being watched, flirting with them with subtle, suggestive movements of her body.

'Marvellous creature,' muttered Ludwig, with a dreamlike smile.

Caspar whispered in Ludwig's good right ear, 'She will be mine!'

Ludwig did not avert his gaze. Something dark and tumultuous suddenly grew within him. He said: 'You would betray me for *that*?'

'Willingly,' grinned Caspar.

Ludwig stared at the woman a long while. Then he spouted, shrilly and contemptuously, 'She can be bought. Look at her! Look at the message she is sending! All such females can be bought.'

The good feeling which had existed among the brothers all afternoon during their tippling and ending with this expedition, evaporated in an instant. Caspar said coldly, 'Ludwig, let me tell you that you are insulting the woman I love. Johanna Reiss is her name, and she is daughter to the respected Reiss, upholsterer. The shop shall be her own. Shall be left to her by her father. You know nothing of her. What are you saying?'

'I see what's going on,' said Ludwig. 'Watch her, brother. Watch her closely. You think she is about her labours. Not so. She is trying to bewitch you. At first it will be all enticements and then – *snap*! The trap shuts. There is always a price to pay. I would never betray you for one of these creatures.'

'You are jealous,' said Caspar. 'You are *always* jealous of everyone.'

'Nonsense. I'm telling you she is a woman I could have *whenever* and *wherever* I wanted. But I have no time for such things.'

'You just have time for countesses.'

'Not whores,' said Beethoven.

'Countesses,' Caspar continued his thought, 'who treat you as a plaything.'

'I tell you,' said Beethoven coldly, 'that girl is a harlot. She will make you miserable.'

They left it there, with bad feelings between them still simmering and volatile. As angry as they both were, they had not quite reached the point, as they had often in the past, where fists would fly. Johann, too, felt angry and hurt at Ludwig's behaviour and silently took the side of his brother Caspar.

'Caspar and I got even,' said Johann, leaning towards Schindler and grinning as he remembered.

Indeed, the two younger Beethoven brothers planned their revenge carefully, using Johanna as their foil. In Baden, where they shared lodgings in the expensive summer resort, Ludwig went to compose in the mornings at a tavern, spreading out his pencils and scores and sketchbooks.

Johanna went there to meet him. Alone. She was dressed like the woman he had imagined when he had seen her just the day before — like a whore. She sat down at his table without being invited, and called for a beer. She stared at him boldly, with her warm, enticing lips glistening, and leaned towards him, reaching for his eyes with hers, until her glass was set before her. She drank it down in a single draught, staring at Beethoven all the while. He laid down his quill.

'Caspar tells me,' said Johanna, with the sweetest of smiles, 'that you are sour as a goat.'

Ludwig heard very little more than static, but attempted to hide his deafness as he so often did now; he nodded and smiled, making an effort to be polite.

'He says that you are famous, but I've never heard of you. Caspar says that's not surprising as your music is too lofty for us ordinary people. In fact he tells me most can't stand it and plenty say it is nothing but a terrible racket.'

Johanna held the empty beer mug between her breasts, seductively.

'Caspar says,' Johanna continued blithely, 'that you treat everybody like a petty tyrant treats his subjects, and that you need bringing down a peg or two.'

And with that, Johanna twisted off the bench and walked away. She gave him a backwards, inviting glance, and went out of the back door, into the tavern's empty garden. Ludwig sat rooted to his seat, staring after her, shocked. Her backwards glance, her smile, the tilt of her head was all the motivation he needed. Muttering to himself, he rushed after her, flinging the door open. She was leaning against the ivy-covered wall.

'Is there something I might do for you?' she asked with feigned innocence.

He moveds toward her, and took hold of her roughly about the waist.

'Not so fast,' she said, wriggling away from him.

Ludwig saw immediately what she was after: he plunged his hand in his pocket and withdrew his purse.

'Forty florins,' he said. 'In gold.'

A smile slowly crossed Johanna's lips and she gradually extended her hand. Ludwig opened the purse and let the coins drop into her palm. Then he pulled her to him bluntly and kissed her on the mouth.

'And that was when Caspar and I got even with Ludwig,' said Johann to Schindler, 'for all his meanness and bullying. Just as he thought he was buying her favours, Caspar and I sneaked in, you see.'

It was a great trick on their famous older brother, and the sole surviving Beethoven brother grinned in remembrance. His face reddened, and he reached for Schindler, and laid a hand on his shoulder with a preternatural grip, as Caspar had done that day to Ludwig.

'My God!' cried Caspar, pretending rage. 'Brother! What is going on here? What are you doing?' He shook a fist in his brother's face, and Johann, beside him, tried to control his laughter.

Ludwig took in instantly the trap that had been set for him and fabricated on the spot an unconvincing lie. 'See?' he said, spinning around and pointing at Johanna. 'Now you have proof, Caspar. I told you what her true profession was. I've saved you from this – this *whore!*'

Johanna slapped him hard across the face. 'Nobody calls me that!' she cried.

And though Caspar gave a harsh laugh, enjoying the joke on his brother, he suddenly became enraged when Ludwig slapped Johanna back harshly, flush on her cheek and jaw. Caspar jumped forwards, pulled his brother around and punched him full in the face. He punched him a second time, bloodied his nose and knocked him down. Ludwig sprang to his feet and charged. The two brothers fell to the floor in a scrambling, wrestling, fist-flaying fight.

'You sanctimonious, full-of-yourself bastard! We got you! We fooled you!' cried Caspar.

Johann looked on with no desire to enter into the fray. He had seen these fights before. In fact, he had been embroiled in them, and had even initiated a few of them himself. He watched Caspar take two fingers in the eyes, and a teeth-rattling punch to the jaw, while managing to deflect a knee to the groin and return one instead. Caspar's nose also started to bleed. Nonetheless, he broke into laughter.

'I fooled you!'

'Fooled me?' cried Ludwig. 'What are you saying?'

Ludwig looked up to find Johanna laughing at him as well. She held aloft the gold coins and sprinkled them on his head, saying, 'Who calls me a whore? Who has the nerve to call me a whore?'

The fighting finally ground down to a halt. Caspar wrapped an arm around Johanna and squeezed her breast and, taking her kerchief, wiped the blood from his nose. 'Yes, who has the nerve to call my love a whore?' He held Johanna close, the two of them laughing.

Young Johann offered Ludwig a mug of beer, for which by way of thanks he took a booting. But Ludwig started to laugh as well. 'A good joke,' he admitted, sourly before breaking into booming laughter. 'A *good* joke!'

***

But there was a serious price to pay for being Ludwig's brother, and such jokes and pranks did not come cheaply. Beethoven may have been a genius but he was also a man, with a man's normal needs. And the combination of his genius and his earthiness had serious consequences for his more mortal siblings.

'He seemed jealous of Johanna,' Johann told Schindler.

'Insanely, stupidly jealous,' laughed Holz. 'Like a bull in heat.'

'He could not bear that either Caspar or I take a wife and lead a normal life,' said Johann. 'It was as though he needed our complete attention, our total commitment and devotion to him. Particularly Caspar. He wanted Caspar under his thumb. And a woman – especially a beautiful woman like Johanna – was a threat. A wife would leave him on his own.'

'And would be a kind of betrayal,' said Schindler, nodding.

'Yes.'

It was as if Beethoven believed that they must both remain, like him, a bachelor. No matter that he chased royal skirts and played suitor and was introduced to the cream of European royalty, while among aristocrats his brothers were simply the butts of bad jokes. No matter that neither Caspar nor Johann was the least devoted to music or had a shred of his talent. And no matter that they had a normal desire to lead their lives their way without his infernal interference.

'When I began living with Therese,' said Johann, 'Ludwig made my life hell.'

Schindler averted his eyes.

Johann studied him. 'I know you detest her,' he said.

'Detest is not the right word,' said Schindler, trying to be diplomatic. But in truth he loathed her and would have happily strangled her.

'But she is my wife.'

'There is nothing I have to say.'

'And I had a right to take a wife,' said Johann.

'Of course you did,' Schindler said.

Withal the woman might be vicious, empty-headed and opportunistic, but Beethoven's behaviour, Schindler had to admit, had been terrible. When Johann began living with Therese, his housekeeper, the arrangement was at first primarily centred around the loins and had not the slightest taint of marital sanctity. But it became more; their affection for each other grew, and Beethoven refused to accept the truth of their relationship. Instead, he threatened Johann with the City Magistracy and applied to the Bishop of Linz. To avoid being expelled from the city, Johann moved quickly to make legal what had been a free union. There was no question that the woman was the scum of the earth, and yet, as far as Schindler could see, she represented the only happiness Johann had ever known.

'But his interference in my life was mild.' Johann bent closer to Schindler and whispered, 'With my brother Caspar, Ludwig's behaviour was worse. Much, much worse.'

Chapter 7

In Flagrante Delicto

Schindler could see now how words could wound even someone as fundamentally thick-skinned and insensitive as Johann. He recalled with something like dismay the unpleasant terms which he and other musicians had used to characterize the brothers: crooked, weak-willed, low-minded, mean-spirited, malevolent, and incapable of any lofty sentiment. They were utterances which aimed at distinguishing Beethoven from his brothers, and rightly so. Nevertheless, Caspar and Johann, no matter how much pain they had created in their dishonest dealings with others, had also been hurt, and were not unaware of it. Johann was doubly excluded: brother to genius, and disliked by all – even, finally, by his genius of a brother. The pain was apparent in the elderly man's inflections of speech, avoidance of gaze and finally by his own words.

'Ludwig loved Caspar more than me,' said Johann, ruefully, grasping his mug in his hands and speaking slowly. 'He loved him to death in those years. It was that way always, really, until the break. For Caspar, Ludwig would move mountains. But when I went off to buy my pharmacy in Linz, Ludwig wouldn't even repay fifteen thousand florins he had borrowed from me.'

'But he loved you both,' said Schindler, somewhat gently. 'I know that. Without saying it in so many words, he made it clear to me.'

'I wouldn't go that far,' said Holz with a sly smile.

'No matter what problems you two may have had,' said Schindler, again ignoring Holz, 'I believe he loved you.'

Johann nodded gravely as though trying to accept Schindler's compliment.

'After Caspar met Johanna,' he continued, his gaze distant, caught up in his recollections, 'she made Ludwig jealous. She took Caspar away from him, I suppose. At that time Caspar and Ludwig lived in Vienna together, you see, sharing an apartment in the Theatre-an-der-Wien, where Beethoven had special dispensation.'

'Caspar worked for Beethoven,' said Schindler.

'He conducted Ludwig's business affairs,' said Johann with a nod. 'But after he took up with Johanna, they fought and argued all the time. Caspar finally couldn't take it anymore. He packed his valise and moved out. A few months later he married Johanna.'

'Did Beethoven not attend the wedding?'

'Wedding?' Johann laughed sourly. 'There was no wedding. Those two eloped. And when Ludwig found out, he refused at first to believe it. The crime was committed while he was away, in fact, but when he came back—'

'Came back from where?' interrupted Schindler.

'From Karlsbad.'

'Karlsbad!' Schindler sat up straight, his senses alerted.

'Yes,' said Johann.

'When was this?' asked Schindler. 'Could it have been 1806?'

Johann nodded. 'I believe that would be right. Or perhaps 1805. I can't recall precisely.' He sighed. 'My memory is not what it once was.'

'Go on,' said Schindler.

'Well, when Ludwig learned about the elopement, all the bitterness and bile surfaced from his belly. He was as jealous as a jilted lover.'

'He was spurned,' observed Holz, 'in a manner of speaking.'

'Please,' said Schindler sharply, not even glancing at Holz. 'Let Johann tell the story.'

News of the elopement had spurred Beethoven to action. He hired a horse, not wanting to wait for the stagecoach, and rode like the wind to the little burg near Baden where Caspar and Johanna were enjoying the conjugal pleasures of marriage, though not as if for the first time. Reaching the town gate, and receiving directions from the watchman, he sought out the village magistrate's office. Ludwig could make a magnificent scene with his fiery presence and, as Caspar related later to Johann, he burst into the old policeman's office and introduced himself with an agitated, 'I am Ludwig van Beethoven and I'm in need of your services!'

Was this a joke? But clearly, judging from the man's

manic state of mind, the mad look in his eyes, it was not. A lowly pair of policemen regarded each other and asked him to sign their register. He did, with a flourish, and they gazed open-mouthed at his signature. Ludwig von Beethoven of Vienna. It suddenly dawned on them whom they were dealing with. The magistrate himself was called, a fat and lazy country bumpkin who fell over himself in haste to scrape and bow before the great musician.

'Noble maestro! I would be honoured to assist you in any way possible.'

'I have come to tell you there is a foul harlot in your town, practising unimaginable debaucheries. She has breasts down to *here*—'

'No! It can't be!'

'It is true, my good man,' said Beethoven magisterially. 'I come from Vienna, a city as sinful as Babylon. Scarcely a man who lives there has not been bewitched once in his life by some evil wench! Oh, I tell you it is too terrible to imagine! Yet, good magistrate, that is no reason why your village should be sullied by the likes of this harlot.'

'On my honour, sir! Yet ... it cannot be!'

'It is, I tell you, and worse. And she has kidnapped my poor, foolish brother. She will ply her filthy trade and rob him blind, and already she has alienated his affections of me and his sense for business for himself. We must banish her from this village and then from this country!'

With the magistrate's ardent help, in no time Ludwig put together a posse of policemen and concerned townspeople. On horseback, looking dishevelled and wild, he led them through the village. When shopkeepers emerged from their establishments to ask what was the matter, they were enlisted on the spot. If there was ever a more motley crew on a mission they considered more noble, it would have been a band of apostles. One member of the mob offered to heat some tar, but the magistrate, however impressionable, was not insane. Grim-faced, curious, fired up with more than a hint of lasciviousness, Beethoven and his followers made their way to the dishonoured door of the house which this disreputable couple had rented for their depraved activities.

The wooden door was bolted. Pounding on it brought no response.

'Break it down,' cried the magistrate. 'Put to it, men!'

The men put their shoulders to the thick wood, probably two centuries old and made to endure the harshest punishment of nature and man. It withstood their battering. A chisel and hammer were immediately applied and a crowbar was put into play. In no time came the crunching sound of success. The door splintered and yawned open.

'They must be on the first floor,' said Ludwig, and he charged up the stairs. He came to a bedroom door and put his weight against it. It was not locked.

Inside, Caspar and Johanna huddled under the bedsheets, a married couple in flagrante delicto. Caught in the act! The sweat of sex glowed on their bodies. An infuriated, astonished Caspar cried to Beethoven, 'Brother! What are you playing at? Are you insane?'

But cowering in their featherbed did no good when Ludwig yanked the cover off. Behind him the townsmen and policemen assembled in the room, their faces agape and red at the sight of Johanna's snow-white charms. She wrapped her arms around her shoulders, trying for a semblance of modesty, and Caspar cupped a hand around his now flaccid member. Still, they were rendered naked by all the probing eyes.

'See!' cried Ludwig. 'What did I tell you? Arrest this woman!'

The policemen inched forwards, uncertain now as to what transpired here. As they drew closer, Caspar moved in front of Johanna to protect her. 'Don't touch her!' he screamed. To Ludwig, he said through clenched teeth, 'This is not funny, brother. I'm going to make you pay for this.'

'Arrest that whore,' insisted Ludwig.

Caspar threw a punch at Beethoven, who retreated towards the fireplace and picked up a poker. He waved it menacingly back and forth, slicing the air. Johanna put a restraining arm on her husband.

'I am no whore,' she said to Ludwig. 'This is slander.'

From the bedside table she held up a document for the police. The magistrate held it close to his eyes, lipreading the words.

'We were married the day before last in Vienna. You can see for yourself,' said Caspar.

'And I am with child,' announced Johanna, with no modesty, even with pride.

Pointedly, she displayed her stomach to Ludwig. There was a distinct mound – suggesting a pregnancy of at least four months.

Ludwig took that in, his face now grey and masklike, as though he realized that after lavishing all the love he possibly could on Caspar, and after putting up with all manner of mischief in business, and so often defending this uncultivated clod of a brother from his aristocratic friends, Caspar felt that he could forsake his brother for a wife. He could and he had. And all Ludwig's fantasies of rescue and return to his version of normality were thus for nought; with them he could perhaps inspire the magistrate and fire up a posse, but he could not, finally, change reality. The real world was not a fairy story, nor was his brother destined to obey his wishes. A current of rage, because there was nothing he could possibly do to thwart this marriage, rushed into him and throbbed in his temples.

'Leave,' cried Johanna testily, drawing up the coverlet over her body. 'Leave, all of you.'

And so they did. They obeyed her, although with no apologies to Caspar and with lingering glances at the beautiful woman beside him. Later there would be time for excuses – for the landlady, delivered as official police business, and the promise of a carpenter to repair the door. For Ludwig van Beethoven, the maestro, there were obsequious explanations, which all boiled down to the simplest: 'They are married, unfortunately, Herr Beethoven. There is nothing that can be done.'

This statement changed nothing in his eyes.

'She is evil,' Ludwig explained to the magistrate in his most commanding manner. And, for the first time but not the last, referring to Mozart's *Magic Flute*, he added, 'That woman is Queen of the Night.'

Caspar's marriage brought an end to any relationship at all between the brothers for the next several years. Beethoven's interference made for a riveting story which would have been more amusing if it did not represent the tragedy of his attempt to control Caspar's life. It did not end in forgiveness, not merely as another fraternal tussle easy to forgive and forget, but rather as a key twist in a great struggle, underladen with volatile emotions which neither Ludwig not Caspar comprehended in the least. Johann finished his tale with a deep sigh and stared at Schindler.

'And, truth to tell, Ludwig behaved no better,' he said, 'when I myself married Therese.'

'I know that story,' said Schindler. 'I know it well.'

'He threatened me with the Bishop of Linz. He came to my house – a house in which I had put him up with a view of the Danube. And how did he repay my hospitality? With a police order requiring that I vacate the city! Ludwig wanted both his brothers under his thumb.'

'That was his temperament,' said Schindler, and he added, 'you were scarcely the only two afflicted.'

'Do you know,' said Johann, leaning closer because now a friendly current, built on beer and confidences, had come to exist between them, 'what it is like to be a shadow? I am a successful apothecary, I am a landowner, I deserve respect. Instead, when I find myself in Vienna, I am ridiculed by all. Why? Because I do not possess the genius of my brother. Is that a crime?'

'No,' said Schindler. 'It's no crime. Not all of us can be geniuses.'

But was it really so hard to understand, he wondered, why Beethoven had reacted so outrageously when his brothers married? He had acted like an enraged mother hen, but then he had denied himself. He had never married. He had been unable to form attachments of consequence with women. He had dedicated himself to his art, which was well and good and could not have been otherwise. But as the eldest brother, he ought to have produced an heir. Instead he had wasted his seed with a series of countesses who would not or could not provide him with an heir, and, as he grew older, with women of corrupted morals. All of this, surely, was of a piece with his relationship with his brothers Johann and Caspar.

Attachments of consequence? Yet there might be one. And if there were, not only was it the estate of Beethoven but his legacy to the world that would be served. Indeed, perhaps his letter to the Immortal Beloved should not have been found wrapped in seven bank notes and bound inside his will. The symbolism suggested one of Beethoven's very weakest characteristics – his willingness to mix money with his notions of women and love. Schindler was determined not to make the same mistake; he could strike at the symbolism by separating the worldly from the loving, in honour of his late master.

'The coach has arrived,' observed Holz, hearing the clatter of horses' hooves outside.

'Wait,' said Schindler.

He opened his bag and withdrew the bundle of bank notes which had come with the will and Beethoven's letter to his Immortal Beloved. Besides, he told himself, he no longer wanted to be pursued by Johann. He no longer wanted to be hounded by the dreadful Holz. He was grateful for Johann's recollections, and thankful he'd had the sense to listen. Now he had a chance to show his gratitude; with Johann, he knew, there was only one way.

'Take this,' he said, tossing the bundle on to the table.

'You're giving up the money?' cried Holz in amazement.

Johann stared at Schindler, puzzlement furrowing his brow.

'It is of no consequence,' Schindler said.

Both men were taken aback. As Schindler rose from the table, donning his frock coat and wrapping his scarf around his neck, Holz said, 'And now you will give up the search?'

Johann was already counting the money – it was amusing to see – and Schindler trained his gaze, reluctantly, on Holz.

'No, I cannot give that up,' he said.

Holz regarded him with a frown.

'I have my reasons,' Schindler continued. 'I will find this lady, the Immortal Beloved. I have no choice. And then she herself will claim her legacy with the full force of the law.'

Chapter 8

Dear, Dear, Dear, Dear Countess

After having dealt with Johann and the unpleasant Karl Holz, it was Schindler's good fortune to soon meet with someone who, like himself, was Beethoven's genuine and dedicated friend. Someone with whom he could talk at length of the master. Someone who had never betrayed him, who loved and admired him, understood his music, countenanced his moods, yet would not put up with his delusions. That person was the Countess Anna Marie Erdody.

He did not even mind the mysterious nature of their encounter, or the fact that it cost him a long journey from Vienna by stage into the hinterlands of Croatia. Although she officially lived in Munich, the countess frequently came to conduct certain business along the Adriatic Coast. His attempts to contact her following the funeral – which she had attended in disguise owing to her political exile – at first went unanswered. But, convinced of his interest in seeing her for reasons which he could not disclose by letter, the countess wrote to Schindler personally and expressed a willingness to meet with him.

The one condition was that he would come to her; she did not wish to return to Vienna; there were too many bitter memories. Besides, she was fearful of being arrested.

The trip gave Schindler sufficient time to sort out his facts, to weigh them up, and try and fit together the history of the Immortal Beloved. Although he had come to no conclusions as to her identity, this much was clear:

It was Countess Julia whom Beethoven once loved, and who wished or imagined that she was the Immortal Beloved.

It was 1806 when, in all probability, the master wrote the letter.

The letter was written perhaps from the environs of Karlsbad, for it was the summer and, according to the testimony of Johann, Beethoven was not in Vienna at the time.

It was soon after that Beethoven returned to Vienna to find his brother Caspar married to Johanna.

Playing the sceptic, Schindler supposed for a moment that the letter was of no significance, nor was the woman to whom it was addressed any more than a figment of Beethoven's fantasy. On the other hand, suppose – even though Schindler had never seen another letter in the master's hand remotely like it – suppose that there *was* an Immortal Beloved, and suppose further that the woman's affections, or

Beethoven's own, had proved chimerical or fleeting. The consequences were clear: in such a case, one would expect that Beethoven's life and work would have remained the same.

But this was not so.

In the years immediately following 1806, Beethoven had composed music that was notably, objectively greater than any work that had gone before or came after. It was his most fertile and productive period. Schindler was astonished when he actually reprised just a few of the masterpieces:

The Fourth Symphony, of 1806, so superbly delicate after the gigantic Eroica; tender and warm, in which the resolution is delayed in a masterful organization of movements. The Fifth Symphony, two years later, with its unbelievable fury and energy, and yet so pure and logical – the culmination of the master's debt to Mozart and Haydn. The Pastoral, Sixth Symphony, so precisely expressive of the beauty of nature – with parts for the quail, the nightingale and the cuckoo – which could never be surpassed for poetry or purity of tone. The Seventh Symphony, with its fine rhythmic propulsiveness, received with great delight by the broadest possible public. The Eighth Symphony, almost humorous but never lacking in poetry and mature thought: more proof of the great variety which the master was capable of lavishing on his audience.

This cornucopia of grand works and more: the Emperor piano concerto; the music he wrote for Goethe's Egmont; the Cello Sonata, written 'amid tears and sorrow', and the Choral Fantasia, with its Ode to Saint-Cecilia...

When music's enchantment reigns
And the poet's words take flight
Then marvellous forms arise
And night and storm turn to light.

One of the grander triumphs, reflected Schindler, from the master's pen in those years was Opus 70. It was comprised of trios for piano, violin and cello, and was dedicated by Beethoven to the person who had helped him selflessly, over many years, and who not only respected his genius but seemed, in some measure, to understand it: The Countess Anna Marie von Erdody – 'My dear, dear, dear, dear Countess' – whom Schindler now stopped in Croatia to see.

He had to take a coach south to Graz, and from there to the old town of Zagreb, where the countess had arranged for a stage to meet him at the old cathedral, at an appointed hour. He was then brought to an inn near the Drava River, in a small village – a sod-covered way station smelling of manure and beer, and filled with rough Hungarian peasants who took him for a German. A high-minded Magyar with a low forehead and a beautiful cluster of large warts beneath his left eye raised a mug of beer when he entered:

'*Egy kaposztaevo.*'

Schindler said clearly and distinctly, 'I am looking for Countess Erdody.'

The peasant looked to a compatriot beside him for an explanation. '*Mit mond?*'

'I am *looking* for the Countess *Erdody,*' Schindler said again, clearly and loudly.

'Ah!' exclaimed the peasant. 'The Kraut said, "I am going to stand you fine people to a drink!"'

The men broke into harsh laughter, and held up their beer steins.

'Yes, of course,' said Schindler, fumbling for his money purse.

Then from the back he heard a woman's voice, delicate and at the same time forceful, used to being obeyed: *'Zolten! Hagyjatok beken az urat!'* And in German, she said, for his benefit, 'Leave the good gentleman alone.'

He turned and she beckoned from where she sat at a rough-hewn table, although set with fine silver and a single candle-lamp, in a dark corner. He tipped his hat to the friendly, mocking peasants and made his way towards her.

'You are looking for someone?' she said, smiling.

'Yes,' he said. 'I am looking for Countess Anna Marie Erdody.' He inclined his head towards her politely. 'And I assume that you are she.'

She offered her hand, half rising from the table but with great effort, using her cane for support. 'Excuse me for not rising,' she said. 'You are Anton Schindler.'

'Yes,' he said, with a bow.

'Please sit and join me.'

She looked pale, perhaps ill, but retained the beauty of delicate, small features, with warm brown eyes and a sculpted jaw. As he kissed her hand, she called out to the watching peasants, *'Latjatok? Egy becsi uriember!'* See? Now here is a Viennese gentleman!' And to Schindler: 'Please don't continue standing there. You make me nervous. You've come just in time for the evening supper.'

They had never actually met, though Schindler knew a great deal about her. In Viennese musical circles the countess was almost a legend. In the 1790s, a beautiful young woman with the most extraordinary lightness about her, who bore herself with every grace, she had hosted musical evenings. The Erdody Palace, where she lived with her husband before their separation, was a grand salon and invitations to her musicales were coveted by the socially elite. This was long before Schindler had even set foot in Vienna, but he knew that it was in her house that the Schuppanzigh quartet played Beethoven's rapturous Trios for the first time. Everyone remembered the countess limping from one pianoforte to the next – and tonight as they sat down to the table, Schindler noticed how her feet were bandaged. She was said to be prey to some sort of intermittent illness contracted long ago upon giving birth to her first child; there were bad periods when she had to be bedridden. But by candlelight a quarter of a century later, even granted all her pain and suffering, she was still the embodiment of warmth and delicate beauty. Just as Schindler had imagined.

'Countess,' he began.

She shook her head impatiently. 'I insist that you call me Anna Marie.' She gestured to the plebeians turned back to their steins. 'These are my people. I am home now. I don't have to play the countess. I can be free.'

He would have preferred to call her countess, but he nodded and said, 'Yes, of course.'

It was surely right and proper, Schindler thought, that the countess's true diadem was the one she received from her people.

Five years ago she had caused a stir heard in Vienna when, somewhere in Croatia, upon her orders, some three hundred peasants asserted her right to a castle owned by her uncle. The uprising underscored the loyalty she inspired, which went quite counter to what was usually engendered by royalty in those parts. Schindler knew little about it, but now facing the woman, he could feel the power of her subtle graces. 'Does Herr Metternich send me greetings?' she asked slyly.

'I wouldn't know,' said Schindler, acknowledging with a wry smile her exile. He knew little about the circumstances, but an anxious Beethoven had spoken to him about her arrest some years ago – was it 1819 or 1820? – an arrest the reasons for which were obscure, perhaps political. In any event, she had been banned from Vienna.

'I was at the funeral,' she said.

'Yes, I know.'

'I had to sneak about like a thief.'

'It was good of you to come,' said Schindler, remembering that she had appeared disguised by a heavy veil. Anna Marie regarded him with a grim smile. 'Poor Ludwig,' she said. 'I miss him so much. Do you, Herr Schindler?'

'Oh, yes,' breathed Schindler. No one since the master's death had thought to ask him, but now he was glad to say it. 'Very much.'

'It was the only time,' said the countess, 'that I have been troubled by my exile. I really didn't care if they caught me. I had to attend the funeral. I owed him that.'

'His death has left a void,' said Schindler. 'For us all.'

'More than that. You will never see his like again. Do they know that in Vienna?'

'Some do,' said Schindler. 'He was not well understood by all. And there were days, I think, when no one understood him.'

'Geniuses seldom are understood,' said Anna Marie. 'Yet the way he was treated ... it disgusted me. Ludwig was too good for them. His fire and his brilliance offended their pea brains.'

'But you and he remained friends.'

'I could match his temperament!' Anna Marie swallowed a glass of brandy and gasped as the harsh liquid hit her stomach. She called the proprietress for another, and ordered one for Schindler as well – *Slivovitz*, plum brandy, she told him, would smooth over any problems connected with the food that would be served to them, or the uncomfortable featherbed in which he would sleep that night.

'I am trying to conclude his affairs,' said Schindler.

'I gathered as much.' She waited for him to continue.

'I ... perhaps ...' Schindler hesitated, not quite certain how to proceed. The countess's delicacy, her genuinely regal manner, made him suddenly cautious, circumspect.

'Out with it,' said Anna Marie, smiling. She added: 'Viennese affairs are seldom concluded with a quill. There always seem to be grave matters of the heart.'

'Exactly. There is a slight question ... well, not slight, in fact. An *important* question. An issue which needs be determined. I ...' Again he paused, struggled for the right words.

'Please, said the countess. 'Be as frank as you need to be. I am not yet an old lady, and I'm not easily shocked. My feet are swollen, I have not spoken to my husband in years, my children are dead all but one. But I am very much alive, appearances to the contrary.'

Schindler breathed deeply and plunged ahead. 'You gave Beethoven rooms at your palace, did you not?'

'Yes, for a time – in my home, actually, for I was separated from the count and had rooms on the Krugerstrasse, in the same residence as the Prince Lichnowsky, Ludwig's patron. I asked him to stay with me. I wanted him near me.'

Schindler told himself that he preferred it this way – the frankness. No need for him to shuffle his feet before Countess Erdody the way he had felt obliged to do with Countess Gallenburg who seemed to favour indirectness, flattery and had managed to socialize the art of seduction. He had always prided himself on his honesty, for getting right to the point – even with the master, the most sensitive and unpredictable of men. When necessary, Schindler had even admonished him to behave decently. *Be fair to your servants and eat the food as soon as the cook brings you your tray, before the maggots get it.* But with women it was another matter. In his experience they usually abjured directness. Nevertheless Countess Erdody had given him an opening; he felt secure about talking to her openly. He now bowed his head, leaned forward and asked, 'Was Beethoven your lover?'

Chapter 9

In Concert

Not an easy question to ask or answer. Fortunately, the worldly and highly experienced Anna Marie Erdody did not laugh out loud, which Schindler feared more than anything else; nor did she shed tears, which he also feared because of the embarrassment it would cause him and the guilt that he had given her pain. Rather, she regarded him steadily and said nothing. *Nothing.*

'I am searching...' he said, flourishing his hands, trying to find the right words.

'For a lover?' Her smile was bright, almost challenging.

'It is not a joking matter,' said Schindler somewhat stiffly. 'I would hope you wouldn't make light of it.'

'I am sorry if I offended you, Herr Schindler.'

He acknowledged her apology with a slight bow. 'It is a question of someone whom he loved ... more deeply and enduringly than ... well, than life itself.'

She laid a hand on his arm. 'You're speaking of someone who was more than just a lover to him.'

'Exactly,' said Schindler. 'An Immortal Beloved. Something grand. Something enduring.'

'Then perhaps I am not the person to ask,' said Anna Marie. 'Would I know if I were? Who could possibly see herself in such an exalted light?'

He debated whether to show her the letter then and there, but realized it would be precipitous on his part. Instead he said, 'If you can tell me what you know, it would be a tremendous help.'

The countess nodded. 'It has several movements, the story of Beethoven and me. Can you understand that?'

'I can,' he said.

'And you must keep in perspective this important thing – Ludwig's isolation. It became greater as he grew older and was overwhelmed by his deafness, but from the earliest time I knew him this isolation of his affected the way he was with others.'

'I'm aware of that,' said Schindler.

What the Countess Julia Gallenburg had stated, Countess Erdody now confirmed: by the time Beethoven was writing the Eroica for Napoleon in 1803, his fame had spread far beyond the Austrian Empire. His works were known and played, especially in England, although, it must be said, many more had heard talk of the master than had actually attended a performance of one of his works. In Vienna, he was prominently discussed.

'Even people without brains,' said the countess, 'people who detested his music, knew that he had genius. Yes, they preferred Haydn and Mozart, who are much easier to understand, and who take their time with you – they explain what they're about But even so, no one could deny Ludwig's genius.'

Schindler smiled. He knew older afficiandos who would tell you all they considered wrong with the Third Symphony – how it was far too long, too complex to be listenable, that finally it must be considered merely noise, nothing more. He recalled how Beethoven's old teacher, Albrechstberger, was reputed to have said before he died, 'Beethoven has never learned anything, and he can do nothing in a decent style.' It stood for the sentiments of many.

'But some of us knew better,' said the countess. 'We revered his music, and waited anxiously for each new work.'

Early in the century, Anna Marie met Beethoven for the first time at the palace of Prince Lobkowitz. She had separated from Count Erdody soon after the birth of her third child, in 1801. The terrible pangs of losing a husband, even a husband that one does not care about, were ameliorated by evening quartets which lasted well into the middle of the night.

'People thought him ugly, but I wasn't one of them. I believed him beautiful,' recalled Anna Marie. 'That summer he took lodgings near my residence in Jedlersee, and finished the Third Symphony. In the afternoons he would walk down by the canal to see me.'

'But you were then...? Ah...' Schindler coughed, clearing his throat.

'We were not then lovers,' said Anna Marie, anticipating his question. 'We had become good friends. At the time he didn't need another lover, I can tell you. I'm sure you know Julia Guicciardi. She filled that role for him.'

'I saw her just three days ago, before leaving Vienna.'

Anna Marie smiled, almost wickedly. 'Perhaps she is this beloved creature – this Immortal Beloved. Even though she married Count Gallenburg, I always had the impression she never stopped loving her "Luigi". He may have felt the same.'

'I don't know,' said Schindler stiffly. 'Perhaps.'

'Ludwig had many love relationships in those days,' said the countess. 'No – that's wrong. I do not mean *love*. I mean *affairs of the heart*. And some were consummated, many not.'

'Did he speak to you about them?' asked Schindler.

'Not every time,' The countess said, smiling, and counting on her fingers. 'He was madly in love with Josephine von Brunswick, who married Baron von Stackelberg. And there was her sister Therese as well – her spinal column was deformed but she was otherwise quite beautiful. Neither could play the piano particularly well. In the case of Julie Vering, he yielded to Stephan von Breuning, and although it gave him pain, he would improvise for this betrothed couple while they sat together into the early hours of the morning. He spoke to me about these and others.'

'But without mention of an Immortal Beloved?'

'Someone immortal to his heart? No. Of course, I have always wondered about the suicide attempt.'

Schindler frowned, surprised 'What? When was that?'

Anna Marie let out a sigh. 'I suppose 1805,' she said, 'or perhaps the following year.'

'Please tell me about it,' said Schindler, alert now, feeling the tension build inside.

'What is there to tell?' said Anna Marie. 'I thought he had left my house in a fit of pique.'

Beethoven had come to Jedlersee, in the suburbs of

Vienna, one day in the summer. And soon after he disappeared.

'I thought something must have happened, perhaps he was offended by some trifle, and had returned to Vienna. But no. After three days he was found in an isolated spot in the garden.'

'He had been there all that time?'

'Without food and nothing to drink but water from the pond. It was all so strange,' said the countess. 'Strange and mysterious. He was contemplating suicide. That much was clear. But he would not talk about it afterwards. Not at first – perhaps not ever, with anyone.'

Schindler sat poker-faced, his hands folded, unable to repress a pang of jealousy that *he* had not known, that the master had not confided in *him*. 'But why?' he said. 'Why would he want to take his life? It seems so out of character. The Beethoven I knew raged at life but he lived in it intensely all the same. What could have been so terrible that it had brought him to the edge?'

'The only clue I have is something he once told me,' said the countess. 'He kept talking about his brother Caspar. "He has married in complete folly," he told me. "My brother has married a woman of the streets!" He was obsessed by it.'

'Ah,' said Schindler, shaking his head, frowning. And then; 'I must confess I don't understand.'

'Nor did I, nor do I now,' said Anna Marie. 'What person decides to commit suicide because of his brother's unfortunate marriage?'

Schindler sat very still, staring ahead at nothing. Suddenly some beautiful words of Goethe coaxed their way into his brain: *When you push your way along the walls, the smooth maple, the sturdy oak and the slender fir tree obstruct your progress with their trunks and roots, and you have to wind your way around them and choose your footing with caution.* What did the words mean? What were they saying to him? Something about Beethoven's fragile state of mind at the time he contemplated taking his life? But try as he might, Schindler could not grasp their meaning.

'You've told me about the others,' Schindler said to the countess. 'But what of you and Beethoven? I don't mean to pry, but these are questions I must ask. I can't tell you how important it is for one to reach the truth. I must carry out this final assignment for the master. Then my duty is done.'

By 1808, the friendship between Countess Erdody and Beethoven was threatening to become something more, although even as they drew closer, more intimate, their relationship was never easy. As Beethoven grew more dependent on her, she became increasingly maternal to him. And as their relationship took on erotic dimensions, they found themselves more frequently in conflict.

'I never claimed to understand his complicated mind,' mused the countess.

'Nor I,' said Schindler.

'But we are not discussing some ignorant peasant or eccentric nobleman,' insisted Anna Marie. 'There are too many of both but very few geniuses. However childish Ludwig might seem with his romances and manoeuvres with young countesses, and his inability to understand the difference between love and infatuation, all that must be considered in light of his whole life. And what he brought to that of all men. There was the music and the tragedy that helped engender it. Neither must be forgotten.'

'I agree,' said Schindler.

'There is what he brought to mankind, and the price he paid. Do you recall the final concert he conducted, at the Theater an der Wien.'

'I was too young,' said Schindler.

Christmastide 1808, Schindler knew, was the occasion of the first performance of the Pastoral Symphony, as well as the C-Minor Symphony, the Choral Fantasia for piano and orchestra, and the Fourth Piano Concerto. It was a fabulous programme, on the greatest stage of Europe, the Theater an der Wien, mounted by Beethoven himself.

'None of the pieces had been performed in public before,' said Schindler.

'But here is what happened,' said the countess, and proceeded to tell him.

Hardly had the great curtains, decorated with scenes from the *Magic Flute*, swept open, scarcely had the first *tutti* chord been struck, than Beethoven jumped up from the keyboard and started to conduct. The orchestra was poorly organized and had come to the concert with too little time for rehearsal. The musicians reading their scores were suddenly confronted with this madman waving his arms wildly. With the first, sudden *sforzando*, the master flung out his arms with such abandon that he knocked over the lamps on the music stand. The audience laughed and Beethoven, casting them a vicious glance, stopped the orchestra. There were uncomfortable titters, then silence.

'Begin again,' he commanded.

Once more the *tutti* chord was struck. Two choir boys were sent by the music hall's director to guard the lamps, which were restored to their place. Once more Beethoven threw out his arms at the *sforzando*, again at the wrong moment. One choir boy ducked. The other received a slap in the face. The audience went berserk with laughter.

'As I watched him,' said Anna Marie, 'I was writhing in an agony of embarrassment. It was a terrible moment for him. And still he did not give up. Again, he hoped to gain respect from the audience and said, "From the beginning."'

But the orchestra by that time was in complete disarray, the audience could scarcely be calmed, and Beethoven himself played an angry chord with such force that he broke some strings on the piano.

'I couldn't stand it anymore,' recounted the countess. 'I hobbled towards the stage. I climbed the narrow, rickety steps, and extended my hand. I hoped my infirmity would annihilate his.'

Beethoven looked up. She was there. Silence descended on the audience. For him, unbearable ringing and buzzing in his ears at such moments drowned out the music and sent him into a state of confusion which could easily be transformed into rage. But Anna Marie was there, tranquil and noble, and he took her hand.

'He was hearing less and less by that time,' said Anna Marie. 'And now the whole world knew of his infirmity. Or would soon know.'

'You took steps after that,' said Schindler. 'Did you not?'

'Yes. Ludwig was unhappy enough with Vienna to contemplate leaving it. The *Musikalische Zeitung* was very unkind about the December concert, and that was merely one of many insults he had endured over the past several years.'

'He received a fine offer from Jerome, the King of Westphalia to serve as Chapelmaster in Kassel,' said Schindler. 'Isn't that so?'

'Yes,' said Anna Marie. 'For five hundred ducats a year – all in *pure gold*. To keep him in Vienna, I convinced the Archduke Rudolph and Princes Kinsky and Lobkowitz that they should pay him the sum of four thousand florins a year as an annuity for life.'

'If only he would stay in Vienna?' Schindler asked.

'Yes. They signed, and he stayed,' said Anna Marie with a touch of pride. 'It was ironic that later on in the same year Jerome's brother should bombard the city.'

'And during the same period, you arranged for a full-time housekeeper for Beethoven.'

'If you had seen his rooms, you would understand. I was appalled the first time I saw them.'

'I've seen them many times since,' said Schindler. 'I certainly can understand.'

'A scene of unbelievable squalor,' said the countess. 'Papers scattered about, half-eaten meals on chairs and divans. Musical scores everywhere, a thick layer of dust on the piano. He could not be trusted to empty his own chamber pot.'

'Believe me, I know,' said Schindler who had emptied it many times.

'In his person, by contrast, he was immaculate,' said Anna Marie. 'He was strikingly clean with his linen, and washed himself constantly, especially his hands. But the disorder in which he lived, worked and slept! You can scarcely imagine.'

On accepting Anna Marie's gift of a housekeeper, Beethoven had said, 'There was one here for a while. She cheated me blind.'

In fact, he had engaged any number of servants, but they had all cheated him, he insisted with hollow laughter.

'You also need an assistant,' Anna Marie told him.

'My brother Caspar was my assistant,' said Beethoven. 'But he has betrayed and deserted me.'

Anna Marie refused to pity him. She said sternly, 'I do not always feel sorry for people. And I do not act like God and make moral judgements. What was between you and your brother I can't hope to understand. I am sure there is fault on both sides.'

Beethoven was taken aback. 'But this woman, this whore, took him from me,' he insisted. 'She trapped him with a child.'

'Perhaps he loves her. Has that ever occurred to you?'

Anna Marie let those words escape her lips without thinking, and Beethoven was outraged. 'But at the same time,' she told Schindler, 'I think he admired me secretly for them.'

'I am sure he did,' agreed Schindler. 'The truth often hurt, but he preferred his medicine bitter.'

Within a short time, Beethoven had moved into the countess's apartments in the Krugerstrasse.

'We had wonderful days and nights,' said the countess. 'I invited the finest musicians. I played the piano and convinced Ludwig to improvise. My children were still all alive and they clung to me like burrs. I would lift them on my knee when I played pedal points. Even when my feet were swelled, life with Beethoven was as rapturous and profound as his music – at least for a time.'

'What happened?' asked Schindler quietly.

'He became quite jealous,' said Anna Marie, 'for reasons that were entirely groundless. He somehow came to believe I was paying one of his servants for sexual favours. It was insanity. He soon moved out, and with his sense of irony, he took lodgings on the Walfischgasse, beneath a brothel. It was two months before I heard from him, and he apologized. He asked forgiveness.'

'Did you forgive him?'

'Of course I forgave him,' said Anna Marie. 'Our story was not quite ended.' She paused, looked thoughtfully into Schindler's eyes. 'But was I his beloved? The answer is, Yes. And the answer is, No.'

The Countess Erdody downed her brandy and ordered another, and one for Schindler as well. 'Do you know about the occupation?' she asked him. 'When Bonaparte pillaged and raped our land and marched into Vienna?'

He shook his head. 'A little. I have read the history.'

'Then let me tell the story,' she said. 'And what it did to Beethoven and me.'

Chapter 10

Siege and Consolation

At long last black bread and meat were served, and Schindler, ravished, could not stop himself from sopping up gravy and wiping greasy fingers on the napkin bibbed to his chest; Countess Erdody barely touched her food. She continued to drink brandy and watched Schindler with a slight smile. Slowly she started to tell him of Beethoven's disillusion with Napoleon Bonaparte.

In the spring of 1809, weeks after Beethoven's concert at Theater an der Wien, Napoleon lay siege to Vienna. 'All of us who had once thought of Bonaparte as a liberator and a force for change now witnessed the truth,' said Anna Marie.

The Beethoven who during the 1790s had called himself a republican – even as he mixed with the declining aristocracy and lived in their palaces – was hardly unusual as an artist and creator. And when, through a rare combination of personal dynamism, military genius, and absurd grandiosity, Napoleon wrested control of the French army and government, Beethoven transferred his allegiance completely, with almost boyish eagerness, to the smallish, intelligent, and slightly insane First Consul. Napoleon briefly embodied to European intelligentsia the idealism of the French Revolution.

'For a time we all believed in him,' said the countess. 'I remember those days, but our admiration took many blows before it was finally extinguished.'

In 1803, Beethoven had resolved to dedicate the Third Symphony, which he was then composing, to Napoleon, as the leader who promised to bring the republican gains of revolution to all of Europe. It was the man himself who inspired him, and Beethoven inscribed on the title page of his score, *Sinfonia Grande, Intitulata Bonaparte*.

'But Bonaparte betrayed us,' said the countess. 'He betrayed a generation. Once he declared himself Emperor he set out to conquer the world. He became a tyrant who sacrificed men and women to some false idea of "The People". He said he brought freedom from the tyranny of kings, but we learned about his lies. He was Saturn gobbling up his children.' The countess shook her head and suddenly looked old. 'Ludwig took Bonaparte's betrayal of our beliefs very hard,' she said. 'His hero, the man he worshipped above all others, had clay feet...'

Countess Erdody took a sip of brandy and continued, saying, 'When Beethoven heard the news that Napoleon intended to have himself crowned Emperor, he scratched out his dedication. I can still remember his words. He said, "Napoleon will sweep aside all human rights and live only for his own vanity and ambition. He will elevate himself above all other people and he will become a tyrant".'

And, thought Schindler, the master's prognostication was a fine one. Napoleon did betray idealism; he did become a despot, a tyrant who sacrificed thousands upon thousands of men and women to some few hollow convictions which meant less and less in the wake of his self-aggrandizement. As his armies marched across Europe he claimed to bring freedom from feudal dynasty, all the while installing his brothers on the thrones of Spain, Naples, and Holland; he replaced the old nobility with a new one, no better, and perhaps crueller, than the old. There were consequences to pay for nearly every inhabitant of Europe.

'Austria suffered the most,' said the countess. 'We always had the secret police to watch for. But when Napoleon crowned himself and his brothers, he ended by making Viennese patriots of us all.

'Whatever his admiration for Austrian culture,' the countess went on, 'Napoleon wanted to accustom the Viennese to eating horsemeat. And he came close to achieving his aim. By 1805 he had defeated the Austrians twice, at Ulm and Austerlitz, and put an end to the third coalition against him. He marched into Vienna late that year, and before he left asked the citizens to pay a fine of thirteen million francs.

'Bonaparte claimed that an army marches on its stomach,' Anna Marie said bitterly. 'What did that mean? His army had the force; they lived off land that wasn't theirs and stole the food. In every village and every town the French passed through they slaughtered the men and raped the women. The peasants had no choice. Robbed of their food and starving, they attacked French stragglers and roasted them whole. Bonaparte made them behave like beasts, inhuman beasts...' She stared at Schindler, her eyes red and swollen with painful memories. 'Beethoven became rabidly anti-French then,' she said. 'And on account of the invasion his *Fidelio* failed miserably, and made him unhappy.'

And yet, Schindler thought, it was ironic justice that the Napoleonic wars had made another Beethoven rich: Johann had realized enormous profits selling tins to the Austrians and supplying medicines to the French. He emerged from the war a wealthy man.

The French soon withdrew from Vienna, but not for long. In the following year, 1806, the Holy Roman Empire ended formally when Francis II abdicated. Europe was ready to be carved up a new way, and Napoleon sharpened his knife in anticipation of the largest share. He was at the pinnacle of his power. By 1809, when Emperor Franz of Austria decided to take back some of what had been his, Napoleon's armies came marching in. They defeated the Austrians at Eckmuhl on the Danube and set their boots in the direction of Vienna – a city which, this time, had determined to defend itself. Under the Archduke Maximillian, some sixteen thousand troops were prepared for battle.

'Much of the royalty left the city,' said Anna Marie. 'Many of Ludwig's friends were among them – Prince Lichnowsky and his family; the Waldsteins; Marie Bigot and her spouse, and Count and Countess Gallenburg. When they tried to escape from Vienna they ran into a column of French soldiers, who dragged them from their cart and stole the jewels lined in Julia's clothes. Apparently, she was raped. We don't talk about it.'

'It was a terrible period.' Schindler shook his head.

'Beethoven wrote his sonata when they left,' said Anna Marie. 'Do you know it?'

He wrote *The Farewell, Vienna, 4th May 1809* for the Archduke Rudolph, Beethoven's highest-born patron, brother to the Emperor Franz. Its fine three movements: *Das Lebewohl*, the sorrowful adagio against the lively rhythm of travel and departure depicting the Archduke's parting from Vienna; *Abwensenheit*, the pain of his absence; and finally *Wiedersehn*, the swift, cheerful and optimistic finale.

'The cannons boomed forth on the eleventh of May,' said the countess, 'two days after the French reached the outskirts of the city. Do you remember?'

'I was still at school,' said Schindler, shaking his head. 'In Moravia. But I remember, because the Archduke Charles was in Bohemia, and it was thought he might advance to Vienna.'

'Yes, we chopped down the trees in the Prater to make barricades in the streets, and we burned the bridges on the Danube and hoped to defend at least part of the city until Charles arrived. But then the French set up their batteries behind the Imperial stables. You had never heard such deafening gunfire. Fires broke out everywhere.'

The sky was ablaze with flames and smoke. It was late at night. Anna Marie retired to her husband's palace to clutch to her bosom her two little girls, Fritzi and Mimi, and her son, August.

'Mimi kept wriggling out of my grasp,' said the countess. 'Even as the windows exploded and smashed.'

The French soon achieved their aim. Napoleon marched into the city and took over the Schonbrunn Palace. Archduke Charles did not arrive; it was only a rumour. In the days that followed, the food shortage was terrible. There was no flour but only barley to bake bread, for the French armies took over the bakeries and fed themselves. They ate the meat and requisitioned the cheese and wine and beer.

'I don't think my poor August ever recovered from the occupation,' said Anna Marie of her son, who had fallen ill. 'In any event, it was not until October that the treaty was signed, and things became easier.' She fell silent, lost in her thoughts.

'And the master,' said Schindler, prompting her on.

'He never stopped composing,' she said. 'And there were beautiful things – the quartet, a concerto and sonata, all in E flat. But you know? From that period what touched me the most was something else.' Anna Marie leaned closer, her gaze beset by longing. Schindler felt a certain discomfiture but did not recoil.

'When my little girl Mimi died, I had not seen Beethoven for some time. When Mimi was buried, he was at the funeral, but we did not speak. I was mourning her loss – I have lost much.'

'I know,' said Schindler in a low voice, forcing himself to meet her gaze.

'But Mimi was the most difficult. My servant came to me and said, "Your highness, there is a peculiar gentleman downstairs."

'I said, "I cannot receive anybody."

'"He insists."

'"Send him away."

'"I have. He will not go."

'"I can see no one."

'"I believe he cannot hear," said my servant, "because he will *not* go away."'

'It was the master,' said Schindler.

'Yes, Beethoven had come to see me. He held a manuscript. I could not speak, nor could he – not until he went to the piano. Then he turned to me and said, "We will speak in music."

'And for over an hour he played.'

Schindler looked for words to ease her remembered pain. 'He consoled you.'

The countess smiled sadly and her eyes brimmed with tears. 'He played the Trio – do you know which one I mean? He had dedicated it to me.'

'In D major?'

'Yes,' she said. '*Ghost*.'

And here the countess turned her head from Schindler and put a hand to her cheek. They sat together without words. Outside, the Drava flowed to the Danube, and then on to Vienna. As though listening to its course, Anton Schindler sat unmoving, not daring to blink. Trying not to feel her pain.

It was quite late now; the sconces were extinguished and the candles burned low. The peasants had disappeared into the night and the proprietress took every opportunity to alert them to the hour. Schindler would remain the night; a room was prepared for him, but he was not yet ready to retire. Nor was the countess.

As they sat talking, they continually refilled their glasses. No matter how much he drank, Schindler made an effort to hold on to his aim as a reporter seeking out the facts, though he could not quite keep his emotions from seeping into his thought and speech. Somewhere between the fifth and the eight glass, however, as he began to feel the effects of the plum brandy, Schindler lost his inhibitions and excessive prudence. He said emotionally, 'You must have loved him very much.'

'With all my heart,' said Anna Marie.

'And he you.'

'No.' She bowed her head, closed her eyes. 'I don't think so.'

'Then he was a fool.'

The sentiment was expressive for Schindler; he downed his glass, feeling flushed and apprehensive that he had overstepped his bounds.

'I like you better drunk,' Anna Marie said with a smile.

'So does all the world.' He gave a short laugh. 'My solemnity can tire people.'

'It is good to speak about Beethoven,' she said. 'Is that why you have come all this way?'

'No.' Schindler shook his head. 'There is more.'

'You said that there is some unfinished business.'

'Yes.'

'How can I help you?'

'Perhaps it is nothing,' he said wearily. 'But then, perhaps it is the key to him. Perhaps others are right and I should let it go. But I cannot. It is impossible for me. I found a letter in his desk. The drawer was all mouldy. The bank notes I gave away. The letter possesses me. I will show it to you tomorrow.' He bowed to the countess as he rose to his feet, weaving slightly.

'Good night, Herr Schindler.'

'Good night,' he said, then hesitated before adding, 'Anna Marie.'

'Yes. Anna Marie. I like that, Herr Schindler. You do listen and you do learn.'

Provided with a candle and a bell, Schindler made his way up the stairs. He could hear music in his head. He could hear the lively *presto* of the Kreutzer Sonata, and as he listened he knew that this was not exactly the end of the day. But rather, its beginning.

Chapter 11

The True Story of the Kreutzer Sonata

Schindler found sleep elusive. He undressed, examined the featherbed for bedbugs, and extinguished the candle. His room was above the kitchen and after he lay down, he listened to the rats scurrying below. In the hall outside, the countess mounted the stairs slowly, painfully, well after he had retired, and he heard her discreet ablutions in the chamber next to his. He doubted that quiet slumber would come easily to her either.

And the Kreutzer Sonata remained with him, its beautiful melodic line, with razor-sharp *presto*, fighting his will to sleep.

In the darkness his thoughts turned to Beethoven. It was still impossible to believe, to accept, that he was dead. It was true, as the Countess Erdody had said that evening, that for all the disorder of his everyday surroundings, Beethoven never neglected his linen. Schindler best remembered him not as he became, untidy in dress, but in a blue frock coat, its brass buttons never fastened, his throat hidden by a neckcloth. And he remembered the master's features at the time they had first met, when his hair was still dark and stuck out at the sides; his squarish face with solid jaw, marked slightly by brownish scars of smallpox, a broad nose, the protruding, defiant lower lip of a sensitive mouth, and, above all, his small, penetrating dark eyes, flashing beneath great bushy brows.

And of the man inside that physical structure, who else but he – surely, he hoped, it would be acknowledged – and a select few others could say they knew that man – proud, headstrong, overly frank, immature, suspicious, mistrustful, unsociable and, to a few, moralizing and high-minded, sometimes to a fault. How could even he really know this man in which such conflicting components came together and were shared in a single temperament?

It was not an idle question. For it held the key, Schindler suspected, to discovering the identity of the Immortal Beloved. Because Beethoven's unique temperament forced you to ask, and to seek an answer for, a single question: how a man can hurt and contaminate for himself the very things he loves the most!

It ran ceaselessly through his head now as he tried to sleep: The Kreutzer Sonata, he realized at length, that represented a fine example of the master at his best and worst, at his greatest and pettiest.

He remembered that it was composed at first for the great mulatto violinist, George Bridgetower – it must have been early in the century, 1802 or thereabouts. The Polish-born son of the footman to Count Esterhazy, a famous Hungarian aristocrat and one of Beethoven's early patrons, Bridgetower exhibited great talent as a young man. When he came to Vienna, he was welcomed by Prince Lichnowsky and the whole of musical aristocracy. And in the prince's salon he met Beethoven; soon the two became close friends. For a time they were constantly seen together, relaxing at Count Deym's, dining with Countess Guicciardi, spending evenings in Taroni's Coffee House. Schindler heard the story directly one day from Bridgewater himself.

'When we played the sonata he was composing,' said the musician, a tall black man of distinguished airs, a gentleman in every respect when they had met in about 1820, in a café, 'I changed the repeat of the first part of the *presto*. Beethoven leaped out of his seat, embraced me, and kissed me on the cheek.'

In a sudden wellspring of inspiration, Beethoven decided to dedicate this new sonata in A major to Bridgetower himself. It was a piece of music that was sure to burn the resin off his bow. The master aimed to complete it for a concert at the Augarten, to be performed with Bridgetower playing in Schuppanzigh's quartet.

'It was all in good fun,' said Bridgetower, nearly two decades later, shaking his head. 'How odd it was.'

As Schindler could confirm, for he had seen the playful dedication, in Italian, on the original autograph score: *Mulattick Sonata. Composed for the mulatto Brischdauere, great composer and lunatick and mulattick.*

And yet, characteristically, soon after the concert and before the sonata was published, Beethoven and Bridgetower had a falling out.

'He became jealous of me, I believe,' said Bridgetower gently, stirring cream into his coffee. 'We shared the attentions of a certain attractive young woman, or at least so he believed. It was a silly quarrel.'

The violinist was not only a superb virtuoso; he was also strapping, handsome, composed, neat, and even-tempered. Beethoven possessed none of those virtues save the first. And he could not stand it. It was not in his nature to be bested by any man.

Therefore, the Bridgetower Sonata was published as the Kreutzer Sonata, dedicated to another violinist whom Beethoven had scarcely met and who, however gracious about it, never in the end played the song himself. And his reluctance was not out of respect for Bridgetower, as the music critics liked to say. The dedication itself was a joke because everyone knew that Rudolph Kreutzer was not capable of playing staccatos with anything approaching Bridgetower's brilliance – and Beethoven's sonata in A major was made up of little else.

It was so often that way with Beethoven: love transformed into hate as fire burns bright in a closed vessel until, at last, all the air is consumed.

Sleep would not come to Schindler; he heard the clock in the village strike two. He uncapped a flask of medicine, which contained some alcohol and which he took for his chronically sore back. He drank a good draught, hoping to slip off into unconsciousness and leave the *presto* of the Kreutzer behind.

But he could not.

His mind suddenly fastened upon himself, upon the case of Anton Schindler – never his favourite subject. Listening to the Kreutzer Sonata, and hearing it play out in his mind now, he was led back in time to review his own life with Beethoven. There seemed to be some connection between the Kreutzer Sonata and his present quest. It was as though by going back in time, by looking at himself and his relationship to the master, he might find a clue that he had overlooked. A key to the Immortal Beloved.

Anton Felix Schindler had gone to Vienna in 1813, just eighteen years old, to study law. But the legal profession was always secondary in his thoughts. He was the son of a musician – the best in the village of Meedl, near Olmutz, in Moravia – and music was embedded in his heart like a vein of crystal in a rock. In 1814, he was given a note from violinist Herr Schuppanzigh to Beethoven, concerning a concert which the former was to give. Young Schindler and the master met, they exchanged pleasantries for a few moments, and though nothing came of it then, Beethoven remembered.

The following year Schindler was arrested and imprisoned for taking part in a student rebellion at the University. It was in reality nothing more than a few meetings of students intrigued by the anti-Bonapartist Carbonari movement, sparking new nationalism; but the government took it seriously, and hunted Schindler down and threw him in jail. After his release, Beethoven sent for him and expressed his strongest support of what he had done. Schindler was nearly moved to tears by the master's concern. And although he lacked Beethoven's fiery personality and was from a different generation, a bond began to develop between them. Soon, they began to meet at taverns, and to go on long walks together.

Their relationship had its ups and downs, it was true, depending on the master's moods, which even then had their wild swings. Trying hard to understand – and forgive – his emotional careenings, Schindler blamed Beethoven's hearing which was truly declining during that period. Schindler remembered him taking up use of the ear horn, and grumbling about it when it proved to be of little help. More and more Beethoven demanded that his interlocutors write down what they had to say to him, using a chalk and slate, or a scrap of paper. It must have been about 1818 when Schindler went down to the booksellers and purchased the first blank note-books, to be used to give some order to the master's conversations. And it was during this period that the firm of John Broadwood of England shipped Beethoven a special grand piano with a tin dome; it was supposed to be an aid in hearing notes with improved clarity, but it only proved to be one more disappointment.

Over the next few years, Schindler was certain, Beethoven experienced a degree of isolation that must be unique in the history of genius. With all these devices to help him hear, none of them brought him the slightest satisfaction. They merely underscored his incapacity, and marked the time until he would be totally without hearing. What good that visitors came and went, Schindler thought, leaving their remarks preserved in a book, and the master confined to his auditory seclusion?

It was in recognition of all that, and not due to some form of toadyism of which he was sometimes accused by his enemies, that Schindler visited Beethoven one day and wrote in the Conversation Book, 'I am working on your piano sonatas.'

Indeed, Schindler had taken up the piano – he was already proficient at the violin – to learn them. Beethoven explained them to him with care, and Schindler went home and practised them until he achieved a level of mastery. He liked to visit Beethoven and be able to say: 'I have memorized another.' It was as though he wanted to become another set of ears for Beethoven. He worked hard between 1818 and 1821, and there came a day when he wrote in the Conversation Book, 'Now I know them all by heart!'

Within a few years Schindler had left the field of law entirely, and was leading the violins at the Josephstadt Theater. And it was then, he felt, that he had become Beethoven's most serious friend, his private secretary, his factotum, his amanuensis. He fetched and carried, he soothed, erred, took reprimand, coaxed, argued, insisted, and despaired. He did it without pay because it was Beethoven.

But was he rewarded?

It was a good question. But for all that Beethoven acted the part of God, and for all the abuse Schindler finally took, for all that the master heaped calumny upon him to others, especially in the last years, Beethoven never lost his essential humanity or his connection to other people. What might appear at first as audacity for its own sake was the working of a soul reaching out for humanity; he laboured in an isolation which was as spiritual as it was auditory, because he had brought music beyond the ken of contemporary understanding.

Again Schindler's thoughts returned to the Kreutzer. When he heard it in concert for the first time, at the palace of Prince Lobkowitz, Beethoven was in the audience. As a welter of conflicting emotions built up inside Schindler, he had the temerity to pass Beethoven a note: *I can't understand it.*

The master, far from flying into a rage, replied, *Neither do those who interpret it or listen to it. But their children might, or their grandchildren. Or their grandchildren's grandchildren.*

It sounded like naked arrogance at first, but Schindler sensed quickly that he had to listen more closely to understand what Beethoven meant. The Kreutzer continued. Beethoven passed Schindler another scrawled note: *Music is a dreadful thing. What is it? I don't understand it. What is music? What does it do?*

Schindler replied: *It exalts the soul.*

And Beethoven could scarcely contain his huge laughter as he replied: *Utter nonsense! If you hear a marching band, is your soul exalted? No, you march. You hear a waltz, you dance. You hear a mass, you take communion. No. It is rather the power of music which carries one directly into the mental state of the composer. The listener has no choice. It is animal magnetism.*

He saw through the whole enterprise, Schindler came to realize, and was capable of putting it into words. Music was saying, according to the master: *This is how it is. Not at all as you are used to thinking and being, but like this. Listen.*

Schindler lay in bed, remembering. No matter that Beethoven had often abused him and caused him much trouble; that was nothing compared to what he, Schindler, owed to him. Beethoven had given him a new awareness of music, an awareness which had brought him great joy. Beethoven's music forced him to see the world in an entirely new light, from a pinnacle of consciousness never before mounted in history. There was no greater gift.

And lying there deep into the night, the violin still scraping furiously in his head, Schindler finally fell asleep. But the master still seemed to stand before him, and he was saying, as though explaining the Kreutzer: '*A man is trying to reach his lover. His carriage has broken down in the rain. Its wheels are stuck in the mud. She will only wait so long. Listen to the sound of his agitation.*'

And Schindler, dozing, recalled a notable passage from one of the master's letters, which, at the time, had meant little to him: *I was warned not to travel at night, told to fear a certain forest, but this only made me eager, and I was in the wrong . . . I remain yours! The gods must send us the rest, whatever has been ordained for us and must be.*

He slept, Faithful Schindler. He thought in a dream: *I remain yours.*

The search for the Immortal Beloved awaited the morning. It was not over.

Chapter 12

Unfinished Business

He slept late, not waking until eight o'clock, long after the maid had knocked and left his basin and pitcher outside the door. The countess limped downstairs even later than he, not until nine-thirty. She had brought to the inn her own plum jelly and it was served to her with thick black bread, which she shared with Schindler. They had strong, sweetened tea, which Anna Marie drank by sucking it through sugar cubes she held between her teeth. Outside it rained steadily, and if it continued for any length of time, the roads would become almost impassable. Schindler was unnaturally anxious, and he knew that it had to do with his eagerness – and part reluctance – to share with the countess what was inside his breast pocket.

'Are you going to show me the letter now?' Anna Marie asked at length.

She gazed at him directly, and in the light of the morning, it was apparent that her desire to think and talk about Beethoven had been stimulated by their conversation the night before. An almost palpable excitation came from her, and Schindler, in addition to feeling anxious, experienced a certain desire to take flight.

'Yes, of course,' he said, almost absently. He drank his tea, and slowly ate some bread and jam. He commented on the beauty of the Drava and the forest beyond, and asked about her uncle's castle, and the land Anna Marie owned in Croatia, and whether she preferred life in exile to life in Vienna which, for Schindler, was already losing its lustre now that the master was gone. Anna Marie, though eager to get on with their business, politely replied to him with full answers which he immediately forgot. Suddenly, his right hand darted inside his coat and withdrew the letter.

'Here, please.'

> *My angel, my all, my other self, just a few words today and that in pencil (yours) . . .*

The countess, looking at those opening words, felt a sudden rush of emotion, a quickening of breath.

'I can't date the letter with exact precision,' said Schindler. 'But reliable testimony puts it in the summer of 1806. It was delivered to a hotel in Karlsbad. How Beethoven recovered it, I have no idea.'

As Anna Marie, reading slowly, finished each page, Schindler took them and read the letter again himself, though by then he had virtually memorized it. No matter how often he read it, he was struck by its hypnotic brilliance and the overpowering need it expressed for this woman – this Immortal Beloved.

Why this deep grief when necessity speaks? Can our love subsist, except by sacrifices, by not asking everything? Can you change the fact that you are not wholly mine – I not wholly yours? O, Lord, gaze at beautiful nature, and resign yourself to what must be. Love demands everything and rightly so; and thus it is for me with you, and for you with me. Only you so easily forget that I must live for both you and me. If we were wholly united, you would feel the pain as little as I do.

'He uses the familiar *Du*,' said Anna Marie, almost absently. 'It was a form he never used in letters to me.'

Schindler nodded, at a loss as to how to respond to that. He said, 'As you can see, he tells of his trouble with the postcoach, of breaking down on a country road. He wrote this from a hotel or a spa.'

The countess continued reading:

My journey was a fearful one; I did not reach here until 4 o'clock yesterday morning. Lacking horses the postcoach chose another route, but what an awful one; at the stage before the last I was warned not to travel at night; I was made fearful of a forest, but that only made me the more eager – and I was wrong. The coach must needs break down on the wretched rood, a bottomless mud road.

Now quickly from the outer to the inner. We will probably see each other soon. I cannot, today, tell you about the observations I have made on my life these few days. Were our hearts ever united I would probably not have had to make them. My heart is overflowing with thoughts that I want to tell you. Oh, I think there are moments when language means nothing ... Be happy! Remain my true, my only love, as I am yours. As for the rest – what is to be for you and me – is in the hands of the Gods.

'That ends the letter proper,' said Schindler as Anna Marie put down the last page. 'But there are two postscripts, or additions. One written in the evening, before he went to bed, when he learned that the mail coach would not depart for three days, and that she, his beloved, would not have his letter before Saturday.'

You are suffering, dearest being (only now do I realize that letters must be posted early in the morning, and that Thursday and Monday are the only days for mail to K.). You are suffering ... Ah, where I am, you are with me; and in talking to you, I am talking to myself. Do what you can, so that I can live with you. What a life! like this! without you, annoyed by the kindness of people here and there, which I neither deserve nor want to deserve. Humility of man to man pains me. And when I consider myself in connection with the universe, what am I, and what is He, whom they call the Greatest? And yet it is herein that lies the divine in man.

'The master is struggling again with what is sacred to him,' Schindler explained. 'Don't you agree? He measures his love against the immensities of the universe. It is a side of the master I saw before only in his music.'

I realize that only on Saturday you will get first news of me. No matter how much you love me, I love you more ... But never hide anything from me ... Good night! I must go to bed. Oh God, so near! so far! Is it not an edifice of heaven, our love? And as firm, too, as the fortress of heaven ...

'Then once again in the morning he wrote her still another postscript,' said Schindler. 'Clearly he was in love in a way he never had been before or would be again.'

Even in bed, my thoughts rush to you, my Immortal Beloved; at times they are happy, then again sad, waiting for fate to fulfill our wishes ...

This last part of the letter provoked such unwanted anxiety in Schindler that he would have preferred to let it go. But he couldn't, and as Anna Marie finished it she, too, was by turns tearful and astonished. He picked it up and read it through yet one more time:

I can live either altogether with you or not at all. Yes, I am determined to wander afar until I can fly into your arms, and make myself quite at home with you, and can send my soul, imbued with you, into the realms of spirits. Yes, thus it must be. You will be resigned, all the more so, since you know how true I am to you. Never will another possess my heart, never, never! Oh God, why must one leave what one loves so much? And yet my life in Vienna, as it now is, is but a poor one, and your love makes me the happiest as well as the most unhappy of men. At this

*period of my life I need uniformity, a certain
regularity; can this exist, our relations being what
they are? My angel, be calm. Only by a calm revision
of our being can we attain our purpose to love
together. Be calm! Love me! Today, yesterday, what
a tearful longing for you, you, you, my life, my all!
Farewell. Oh, continue to love me! Never misunderstand the truest heart of your beloved Ludwig.
Eternally yours. Eternally mine. Eternally we ...*

Schindler laid down the letter. 'Tell me what you
think, frankly,' he asked the countess.

Anna Marie said nothing at first; she rose from her
chair. 'We need more tea,' she said, and hobbled into the
kitchen. He heard her, a moment later, engaging the
proprietress in a heated debate over the proper strength
of tea. She's nervous, Schindler thought. The letter has
left her stunned. Returning to the table, she sat down,
glancing at Schindler, but silent. When the tea was
brought, she sipped at it, once more through sugar cubes
in her teeth. He was impatient and for a time said
nothing, but then burst out, saying, 'Tell me, Countess –
Anna Marie – do you know who she is?'

Countess Erdody set down her teacup so shakily that
she nearly broke it. 'Why is it you think I should know?'
Her manner was strained and fragile.

Schindler, taken aback, said, 'I'm sorry, I—'

She leaned close and interrupted, saying, 'You tell me
you want to know the identity of this Immortal Beloved.
Well, perhaps you do and perhaps you don't. But in any
event, you shall never comprehend anything if we don't
take up once more and finish what we undertook last
night. Do you understand that?'

'Of course,' said Schindler, slightly bewildered.

'Now let us begin again. Where we left off.'

'Of course.'

'Perhaps you recall a certain incident that took place between Ludwig and his brother Caspar. One that involved the possible theft of Beethoven's music.'

Schindler nodded. 'I remember. There is no way I could possibly forget.'

'That is where we must start.'

'I don't understand.'

'You will.'

She wanted to know about a stormy encounter between Beethoven and his brother, and insisted that he recount to her the entire story. Although it seemed to him absurd, truly, the countess had become suddenly so edgy and temperamental that he did not question her any more closely, but did as she said.

'It was 1815, was it not?'

'The dead of winter,' Schindler answered.

For a few years following his marriage, Caspar Beethoven and brother Ludwig had not been on speaking terms. Beethoven's jealousy and his disgraceful intrusion upon Caspar and Johanna during their honeymoon had poisoned their relationship; they could scarcely bear to be in one another's presence. But they had reconciled partially in 1809. At the time of Bonaparte's invasion of Vienna, Beethoven's apartments were on the ramparts of the city, and he was vulnerable to direct cannon fire. So he took up Caspar's invitation to stay with him in his home in the Rauhensteingasse. There Beethoven cringed in the cellar during the bombardment, holding pillows to his ears, fearful that the roar of the cannon would further damage his hearing.

'This was not, however, a complete reconciliation – for one thing, Beethoven refused to speak to Johanna, and in fact never saw her or her son while he stayed there during the bombardment. But after a few years more, the two brothers began seeing each other regularly,' said Schindler. 'But always at Beethoven's apartments. Caspar once more took to handling some of the master's business affairs.'

'I remember that all Ludwig's Viennese friends were against Caspar,' said Anna Marie. 'When his name came up, it was invariably with a grimace and an irritated sigh. Everyone except Beethoven spoke of Caspar as foolish, ineffectual, and childish.'

'I must confess I thought him a fool,' said Schindler.

'And so perhaps he was,' said Anna Marie. 'The Viennese can be extremely hard on certain individuals who lack culture, and Caspar was one.'

Schindler only recently had begun to see Beethoven on an almost daily basis, to carry out small errands and tasks. He was glad to do anything he was asked just to be in contact with the master; indeed, he was still awestruck in his presence, and astonished at the man's daily routine. Beethoven worked and reworked his scores with unimaginable diligence, and Schindler witnessed this magnificent creative process first hand. That out of the chaos of Beethoven's everyday surroundings came such beauty, Schindler found remarkable in itself. Beethoven rose early in the morning, about dawn, and went directly to his work desk. He would not leave it, except for short breaks, until two or three in the afternoon. Then, after he ate his dinner, late in the afternoon, he took long walks all over Vienna. As he walked he worked over material in his head, hummed aloud oblivious to the outside world, his sketchbook and a carpenter's pencil in the pocket of his coat, ready if an idea occurred to him. When Schindler would question him about his working methods, Beethoven would respond fully and generously, giving the grateful Schindler new insights into the great composer's mind.

At the same time, Schindler could not help but notice another side to the master, what he came to think of as the dark and evil side. One day Schindler arrived to find that Beethoven could not find some sketches he had written. He had worked himself up into a frenzy of frustration and had started to accuse the washerwoman of having taken them. The old woman, who had known Beethoven scarcely a week (and was never to be seen again) had already started to sob, protesting her innocence in the strongest terms. Schindler calmed her and sent her away, and turned to Beethoven, appealing to common sense.

'What use would a washerwoman have with your sketches?' he asked. And gently joking, he added, 'Only you can decipher them.'

'You don't know,' said Beethoven bitterly. 'That hag could have sold them as souvenirs.'

'I doubt that very seriously, Master.'

Beethoven sat at his desk, deep in angry thought, as though engaged in a heated discourse with himself. Then suddenly he jumped up and cried, 'You are right! Now I remember!'

'What?'

'Caspar has them!'

'Ah!' said Schindler, relieved. 'So the mystery is solved. Do you want me to go fetch them for you?'

'I shall go,' said Beethoven. He donned his frock coat. 'I left the sketches in Caspar's safekeeping. He should have returned them to me long ago.'

Schindler's intuition told him that he should accompany Beethoven to his brother's house. He sensed that all was not well. He realized it was not surprising that Beethoven, who lived in such perpetual disorder, and who seemed to change his residence every few months, consigned his manuscripts to others' safekeeping. But something had launched an air of suspicion and mistrust in Beethoven that day, and, for reasons he could not divine, Schindler sensed in him a rising tide of rage. His mouth was set, his lower lip stuck out angrily; he walked with no consideration for others, paying attention only to horse droppings and puddles. Reaching Caspar's house on the outskirts of the city, Beethoven pounded sharply on the door; when it was not opened in an instant, he burst inside. The family was in the kitchen, at dinner.

'My God!' exclaimed an astonished Caspar. Schindler followed reluctantly, and bowed stiffly to Johanna, whom Beethoven ignored. It had been many years since they had last seen each other, not since Beethoven had burst in on their honeymoon when she was four months with child. But Beethoven was casual in his dismissal of her, as though he had just seen her that morning. Their son, Karl, a pleasant-looking, brown-haired lad, perhaps nine or ten, put down his spoon and stared at the agitated figure in wonder.

'Are you my uncle?' he asked. 'My Uncle Ludwig is a famous composer.'

Beethoven, caught off guard, broke into a warm smile. 'Are you Karl?'

The boy nodded. 'Yes. And I am taking music lessons.'

'What's the matter, Ludwig?' asked Caspar suspiciously. 'What brings you here?'

'Herr Schindler,' said Beethoven, with a touch of sarcasm, 'allow me to introduce you to my good brother Caspar, and my fine nephew Karl.' Johanna went unmentioned.

'It's always good to see you,' said Caspar, 'but as you can see, we are eating dinner just now.'

'I need the sketches I entrusted to you,' said Beethoven.

'They were all returned to you,' replied Caspar. 'As you ought to remember.'

'They were not,' said Beethoven, raising his voice, 'and I need them.'

Caspar regarded his brother with a mixture of anger and fear. 'Ludwig,' he said warningly.

'The sketches!' spat Beethoven. 'Otherwise do you think I'd step foot in this house with her here?' He still did not glance in Johanna's direction.

He suddenly marched out of the kitchen. After a moment of shock and indecision, Caspar, followed by Johanna, Schindler, and then Karl, went after him. When they found him, in the study, he was flinging open drawers and riffling through their contents, strewing papers and books on the floor. Caspar took him by the shoulders.

'Brother, I said your papers are not here!'

'They are!' Beethoven screamed. 'You have them! *I want them!*'

His eyes finally fell on Johanna and he pointed at her,

accusingly. '*You*.' There was a shocking depth of scorn in his voice.

'Please, Master.' Schindler made a feeble attempt to intervene. 'This is not civilized behaviour.'

Johanna stepped forward. 'If you want to cause a scene, I would rather you did not do it in front of the boy.'

Beethoven pretended not to hear. 'What did the whore say?'

'Maestro, I beg you,' said Schindler.

Caspar suddenly pushed his brother hard on the chest and cried: 'Get out of my house! *Get out!*'

'You have destroyed them, haven't you? You've thrown out my music!' With a gesture towards Johanna, he added, 'You and this foul strumpet you call a wife.'

Taking up a chair, Caspar swung it clumsily at Beethoven and without much force. It knocked him backwards, but then he quickly lunged at Caspar and wrestled him to the floor where they were locked in a vicious embrace. Schindler, with no taste for violence, tried vainly to pull the two men apart. Beethoven by then had Caspar by the neck and was banging his head against the stone floor. Schindler saw a spray of blood, he wasn't sure from whom, and heard Johanna scream; the boy began to weep.

'You betrayed me!' cried Beethoven hoarsely.

It was Johanna, finally, who made them stop. Caspar still struggled, but more feebly, while Beethoven still howled with rage. She took a scrap of paper, wrote something on it, and thrust it in front of Beethoven. With a horrible frown, he looked from the note to her. She was saying, over and over, 'Ludwig! Caspar is sick!'

And Beethoven, looking down at his brother, could see the truth of it. Caspar was having a spasm of coughing. Dark blood and sputum had spurted out of his mouth and spattered Beethoven's front.

Beethoven knelt by Caspar, his face a mask of bewilderment and sudden hopeless regret. Abruptly, he let out a sob and cried, 'My God! Forgive me, brother! I'm so sorry!' And he attempted, with an astonishing rebirth of affection, to take Caspar in his arms. Johanna pushed him roughly away, and put a handkerchief to her husband's mouth as he coughed up more dark sputum. To Beethoven she said quietly but with deadly force, 'Leave our house, Ludwig. Now. And don't you ever return here.'

Schindler picked up the note she had written. It read: *He has consumption.*

'It is an unpleasant story,' said Schindler to the countess. 'And I really don't see what possible connection it has to Beethoven's letter. I just don't see it.'

'You must go on, Herr Schindler,' she said. 'There's an answer if only you look hard enough.' Schindler knew that she was right. He had come this far; he knew that he was incapable of dropping the search. He only hoped that his researches would reveal some secret, unrequited love that could be fitted happily into Beethoven's life and the general conception of him in the world at large. But he was beginning to suspect that this would not be – that the Immortal Beloved would perhaps be an embarrassment to the master's memory – and although he was, to some extent, frightened by this, he knew that the Countess Erdody was right. There was no choice but to continue the quest wherever it might lead.

Chapter 13

At War with the Queen of the Night

Caspar's fatal illness raised the curtain upon a tragedy that occupied the master for fully five years, with consequences long after, in which Beethoven attempted to wrest control of his nephew Karl from the boy's mother, Johanna. To understand *why* he did this – what compelled him to draw so close to a small boy he had paid scarce attention to until his brother lay dying – would require the insight of a psychologist. Schindler had always felt immensely frustrated by the whole affair, and he shook his head and said to Countess Erdody, 'It is still a great mystery to me. Why did he want Karl? The master never showed any inclination to like children or to care about an heir.'

She nodded. 'Yes, and that is why it is important.'

'Of course he could have changed,' said Schindler. 'The boy *was* the only Beethoven left in the world. Johann has no children. Perhaps that was his motivation.

After all, a man grows old and begins to worry about mortality.'

'Yes, but would that explain why he treated Johanna so monstrously?'

'I'm afraid nothing would explain that,' said Schindler.

Anna Marie leaned close. '*Nothing*? Don't be so sure.'

As Caspar's illness led painfully to his death over the next six months, no brother could be more solicitous than Ludwig. For all they had fought in the past, for all the turbulence, no one could doubt Beethoven's love. Meeting Caspar one morning on the Ferdinandsbrucke, Ludwig wrapped his arms around him and covered him with kisses, to the amazement of passersby. Although he had become decidedly stingy as he grew older, Beethoven sent money so that his ill brother might have a carriage at his disposal. He arranged for the sale of Caspar's fine pipe bowl. He even sent letters to the Ursuline nuns in Graz, requesting peacocks for Caspar; indeed, those beautiful birds were duly received and strutted around his property and became part of his final estate.

'Ludwig's mother also died of consumption,' Anna Marie told Schindler. 'It was as though Caspar's illness brought back to him all of his emotions connected to her.'

'If it had stopped there, all would have been well,' said Schindler. 'But can you tell me why this terrible rage against Johanna?' The why of it still rankled him.

'It became a battle which was long and tortured,' she offered.

'Long and tortured?' said Schindler. 'That scarcely half describes it!'

'We all remember the essentials,' said the countess. She paused and then added, 'Do you recall what the philosopher Hegel said?'

'He said many things.'

'Yes, but this is apropos. "To grasp anatomy," he said, "one must familiarize oneself with each of the bones, not just gaze upon the body".'

She was right, of course. It was useless to recoil at Beethoven's behaviour, which everyone would agree was far from appropriate. But there had to be reasons for what he had done – even if hidden from himself – and reasons for what the others had done, no better understood perhaps. One had to look closely at Johanna – good mother or whore? And at Karl – sweet little boy or insufferable brat? And at Beethoven – loving uncle or monstrous usurper? There was no simple perspective from which to form a clear, objective understanding of their motivations. Still, that was the task Schindler had set himself. And perhaps if he could plumb the motivations to their depths, he would come closer to learning the identity of the Immortal Beloved.

'What about Johanna?' said the countess. 'What would you say of her?'

'I see her as a mixture of qualities,' said Schindler. 'Certainly frivolous. And she's an impractical person. She does not always know how to tell the honest from the dishonest deed. I doubt she understands the notion of honour. She stole money from her husband once long ago, and was arrested and compelled to give it back. And she enjoys parties. She may have had a lover.'

'Every woman in Vienna had a lover,' said the countess dismissively.

Schindler coloured and immediately tried to amend his righteous tone. 'I didn't mean to judge.'

'We all judge,' said the countess. 'And what do you make of Karl?'

'He was an intelligent boy,' said Schindler. 'And may become a reasonable man who can take his place in society. But as a child he was manipulative, and as a young man he preferred gambling to school, and, well, frankly I have come to loathe him. But then, it is all a tragedy.'

'A tragedy in how many acts?' asked the countess.

'Too many,' Schindler answered.

'Begin with the first.'

'There was the will ,' Schindler said.

As he lay dying, Caspar made out a will that granted Beethoven co-guardianship of his only child Karl. This was Beethoven's idea and no doubt Caspar's wish, given the master's substantial long-term financial prospects. Caspar wrote that he hoped his brother would 'bestow love and friendship' upon his son Karl, and expected him to do so because Ludwig 'has often aided me with true brotherly love in the most magnanimous and noblest manner'.

'Yet just before he died, there was the codicil,' added Schindler.

'Johanna was afraid,' said the countess, nodding. 'So was Caspar.'

Indeed, racked by terrible coughing, and spitting up blood, Caspar added to his will a supplementary document stating that he did not want Beethoven to take Karl away from Johanna, or take sole charge of the education and upbringing of the child. Caspar's fear – and his reason for modifying the will – stemmed from the hatred his wife and his brother seemed to feel for each other. *'God permit them to be harmonious for the sake of my child's welfare,'* he added to the codicil. *'This is the last wish of the dying husband and brother.'*

'And soon after, Caspar died,' said the countess. 'God rest his soul.'

'He was a mean, petty, ignorant, and often unpleasant man,' said Schindler. 'He beat his wife and stabbed her once in the hand, and was capable of conducting himself like a pig.'

'Let's move to the second act of the tragedy,' said the countess, gently leading Schindler onwards.

'It would be the funeral and its aftermath,' Schindler answered.

Even before Caspar was in the ground, Beethoven had undertaken his campaign to take Karl away from his mother. Schindler recalled the day of the interment: 16 November 1815, at the Wahring Cemetery in Vienna. Schindler was there with the master, and as the priest read the liturgy, he felt at once a sense of relief and of guilty satisfaction that Caspar Beethoven was about to be lowered into the earth. The previous months' concern with his enfeebled brother had taken Beethoven away from his work and obsessed him. Now, Schindler thought, there would be an end to it; order could be restored to the master's life, and hence to his own.

But even before the ceremony was finished, Beethoven was bristling with anger, and staring pointedly at a poorly dressed man who accompanied Johanna. He watched closely as this mourner comforted her and led her away with an arm around her shoulders. Much to Schindler's surprise, Beethoven tugged on his arm, and in a cruel, harsh whisper said, 'See that man? His name is Jacob Raicz.'

'A roomer in their house if I'm not mistaken,' said Schindler.

'Yes. And do you see? My brother's bed is not yet cold and Raicz is already climbing in.'

There was not a single iota of evidence for such an assertion, of course. Was Johanna capable of it? Schindler had no idea. He did wonder, however, at the master's treatment of her, which he considered more pathological than malicious. Instead of comforting her on the day of his dead brother's funeral, Beethoven was vilifying her. His attitude seemed almost beyond hatred.

Within two weeks of Caspar's death, Beethoven launched his assault against his sister-in-law. He asked the Austrian Imperial Landrecht, the court of recourse for the nobility, to grant him sole guardianship of his nephew Karl. He produced weighty reasons for this usurpation – considerations such as that the mother was a whore.

The battle was joined.

'The Landrecht was predisposed to accept Beethoven and rule in his favour,' said the countess, 'as one of noble blood – or so he had long portrayed himself. Many of us knew, or suspected, differently.'

Six weeks later Beethoven stood beneath the majestic chandeliers in the Imperial Palace to 'vow with solemn handgrasp' that he would perform his parental duties with regard to Karl. He became sole guardian, removed the boy from his mother's home and placed him in a private school.

'He would have taken the boy to live with him right away,' said Schindler, 'but the judicious among us pointed out that the intolerable state of his lodgings forbade such a possibility. He was forced to agree, for the time being.'

'That was when he wrote to me,' said Anna Marie.

'Overcome with joy, I imagine,' said Schindler.

'He told me, "I have fought a battle for the purpose of wresting a poor, unhappy child from the clutches of his unworthy mother, and I have won the day. *Te Deum laudamus*".'

The whole affair was monstrous already – and motivated not out of love of the child or loyalty to Caspar's memory. It was revenge, thought Schindler, pure and simple: revenge on Johanna. And if Beethoven had been an ordinary mortal, Schindler would never have set foot again in the master's apartments. But for all his evil ways, Beethoven was a god to Schindler and he stayed near at hand, ever the helpful factotum, even though Beethoven cooled to him for a time after he advised against adopting Karl.

Having removed Karl from Johanna's home, Beethoven undertook a campaign to stigmatize Johanna as a woman of base morals, unfit to be a mother. He made every effort to keep her from seeing her son at all. For her part, Johanna fought back with every means at her disposal. She went to Karl's school every day, and during his free periods brought him to her house in a cab. Beethoven tried to put a stop to these fleeting visits as well by writing the most outrageous letters to the headmaster of the school.

'The Queen of the Night was at the Artist's Ball until three o'clock in the morning, exposing not only her

mentality but also her body – for twenty florins, people whispered, she was to be had! Oh, horrible!'

Beethoven petitioned the court to 'exclude the widow' from all direct communication with Karl; and though he won the day at first, these early skirmishes signified only the beginning of a long struggle, because Johanna fought back.

'Beethoven wanted to dedicate himself to Karl,' said Schindler. 'He called himself Karl's "trouser button". But I think he underestimated Johanna's powerful commitment to her son.'

'One evening, soon after Caspar's death,' said the countess, 'I invited them to come to hear Schuppanzigh perform with his quartet. Ludwig arrived with the boy and they sat together. He stroked the boy's hair throughout, and Karl was lost in the music, as though in a dream. Ludwig's eyes shone with joy when he looked at him. All the love in his rich and deep nature seemed to focus on this child. He may have been his uncle, but there was no more tender father in creation.'

A short time later Karl did go to live with Beethoven. Schindler recalled that mountains were moved in anticipation of his arrival. Beethoven bought furniture, had his rooms tidied up, engaged new servants, swore off bad habits and turned himself into a sort of mother hen. He made a bedroom for Karl, with a clean featherbed and a new washstand.

'It's getting colder, Frau Frolich,' he told the new housekeeper. 'Are two blankets enough for Karl?'

And in the kitchen over the stove, he looked into the pot, where a fragrant stew bubbled.

'You made it thick?' he demanded.

She nodded vigorously.

'His mother did not feed him properly. We must build him up.'

She nodded more vigorously, shaking her head. The poor woman was forced to write answers to a hundred questions of household detail which Beethoven had posed in anticipation of Karl's settling in.

But yes, the countess was right. A supreme look of joy would soften Beethoven's features when he gazed upon Karl. He was, at first, endlessly indulgent. Over dinner they held most of their conversations on scraps of paper, for by then Beethoven's hearing was so seriously impaired that he could not hear even when one shouted in his ear. Schindler had witnessed some of these dialogues, and read parts of others, and there was on the master's side a newfound delight in recounting his life. And Karl, at ten, was old enough to understand, but too young to feel the weight of, his uncle's need to control his life.

'You shall be a musician,' Beethoven told Karl.

'I want to be a soldier,' Karl replied.

'You shall be a composer,' said Beethoven, undaunted.

'No,' said Karl with good-humoured stubbornness. 'A soldier.' He mimicked firing a gun.

'When I was your age,' said Beethoven, 'I gave my first concert. I was terrible! Your grandfather thought that he was going to make a fortune out of me as a child prodigy. Like Mozart!' He touched the boy's cheek. 'I would never do to you what was done to me.'

He would not, that is, come home drunk at midnight and drag an eight-year-old boy from his bed and force him to play scales until dawn; he would not box the boy's ears or slap his hands when he made a mistake. He would not present a twelve-year-old boy in concert, pretending he was nine; nor would he beat him within an inch of his life when he failed to match Mozart's prowess.

'My dear mother died of consumption,' Beethoven told his ward, 'as did your papa.' And embracing Karl he said, 'Your papa I loved most of all.'

At the beginning uncle and nephew were infatuated by each other, and there was every reason to believe that the living arrangement could be salutary for both of them. But Beethoven was not satisfied with that. He could not simply accept his role as good uncle to a nephew who was – at least before he became a pawn in a ridiculous and terrible battle from which no one could emerge victorious – a decent boy. A boy who did well in his Greek and could do sums, unlike Beethoven, and who even knew how to spell.

Schindler wondered why Beethoven couldn't be satisfied being a good uncle instead of a dreadful father – one who, when Karl asked the question, 'Why is Mama bad?' replied, 'Do you know what a harlot is?'

Frivolous, lax, headstrong, malicious. Odious and evil. That was Johanna, according to Beethoven.

'It was not worthy of him,' said Schindler. 'His anger, yes, perhaps, for a man such as he knows the sublime rage of nature. But it all proved to be so destructive.'

Beethoven wrote a letter to the Court, the writing of which Schindler refused to be a part of in any way:

Immediately after the death of my brother, she was in secret commerce with a lover, through which alone the innocent modesty of her son was injured. She was to be found on all dance floors and at merrymakings, while her son had not even what is needed and was left alone by her with a miserable maid.

She even tried to lead him astray with money and gave him money to abuse other people for her evil ends ... Me, his benefactor, support and stay, in short his father in the true sense of the word, she attempted to vilify by the most abominable intrigues, cabals, slanders, and to infuse her moral poison into all, even the most innocent.

'Yes,' said Anna Marie. 'He wrote me a long letter around that time. He felt he truly had become the real corporeal father of Karl.'

'It was all a kind of hopeless fantasy,' said Schindler.

Anna Marie lowered her head. 'But not the rage,' she said. 'Not the rage.'

'No,' agreed Schindler. 'And the worst was yet to come.'

Chapter 14

The Promise of a Grand Oratorio

The master was often angry with Schindler in those years, and Schindler willingly kept a distance from Beethoven's legal efforts to control his nephew. But their strained relationship never led to a break. Beethoven needed him, and because he loved the master, Schindler remained close at hand and did as he was asked. If he did not get along with the rest of the entourage of 'friends', it was because of his honesty. He did not spy and tell tales, like the wretched Holz, and if the master asked his opinion he was incapable of tailoring it to please him.

But he was by no means pure. Schindler even carried out a mission for Beethoven to warn Johanna that the master was aware of certain of her deceitful tactics. Schindler met her on neutral territory in a café; she came dressed in black and attempted to be frosty in appearance, although she could not rein in her sensuality. Whether it was the curve of her bosom or the gaze of her liquid eyes, he didn't know, but even Schindler was stirred. She indeed retained an appealing beauty, and if she was not Queen of the Night, he thought, the night could have done much worse.

'It has come to our attention,' he told her, 'that you have been bribing the master's servants in order to have access to Karl in secret. And yet you well know that Beethoven would allow certain visitations under the agreement of the court.'

This was not strictly true; Beethoven was then doing all he could to prevent Johanna visitation rights. She responded with venom, saying, 'What new insanity is this? He has made it all but impossible for me to see Karl.'

'He respects the court's decision.'

'You are talking about my son,' Johanna cried. 'My *son*, whom I have not seen for a year. My son, who is being taught to hate me.'

'The decree of the court states—'

'I know what it states,' she interrupted angrily. 'Can you look me in the eye and tell me that a mother has no right to see her son? *Can you?*'

He was silent.

'I will fight this,' she said. 'I am fighting it already.'

The situation was not helped by the fact that as soon as Beethoven took Karl to live with him and kept him from seeing his mother, the boy rebelled. He revolted instinctively, without rancour, without knowing fully why. But it should have been clear to the master, Schindler thought, that a boy wants his mother. After being mildly scolded by Beethoven – his real father, Caspar, used to whip him with a belt – young Karl once ran away to Johanna's. Thus encouraged to counter-attack, she petitioned the court to relieve Beethoven of his guardianship. Schindler did not doubt that the boy's complete absence from her life was intolerable to her, and it was not surprising that she had bribed Beethoven's servants with stores of coffee and tea for a few minutes with him. What mother would act differently?

And now all of Beethoven's eccentricities were employed as weapons by Johanna when she went the next time to court. It was not only for fleeting moments with her son that she had been bribing the servants, but to gather damning information on Beethoven's habits and way of life. Johanna would fight Beethoven much as he had fought with his brothers Caspar and Johann and they with him – using tactics that were dirty and devious.

She hired one of her relatives, Jacob Hotschevar, as her lawyer. It was a propitious move, because Hotschevar proved to be a highly proficient lawyer who wrote his briefs in the finest German legalese. In his superb arguments, he earned many points for Johanna. He said of the Beethoven brothers that 'their excellent qualities notwithstanding, all three of them are eccentric minds'. One could see the justices heaving a collective sigh of assent. 'This truthful and frank statement cannot detract from the honour of Messrs van Beethoven,' Hotschevar went on, 'but it does prove incontrovertibly that, overpowered by their temperaments, they do not in all their actions and undertakings set to work with the requisite circumspection and calm dispassion.'

Calm dispassion? Housekeeper Nanette *has changed completely since I threw those half dozen books at her head*, wrote Beethoven in a letter which Schindler copied. *Presumably some portion of them has entered her brain or forced their way into her evil heart, so at least now we have a bosomy traitress who steals me blind!* Then there was the time when Beethoven threw a chair at another poor Fraulein, and Schindler stamped his feet in protest.

'You *cannot* act in this fashion, master!' cried Schindler. 'I won't allow it. It's completely uncivilized and barbarous.'

'I am that which is,' laughed Beethoven, citing one of his favourite sayings from Egyptian myth.

'And I am leaving,' said Schindler.

But he always returned. He was with the master, in court, when the worst of this sort of behaviour came back to haunt him. One of those abused servants appeared before the magistrates, dressed in her Sunday best. She had an honest face and was quicker to bleed from an insult than one might have imagined. Schindler was busy that morning transcribing furiously so that Beethoven could follow the testimony of Frau Frolich, as she was interrogated by Jacob Hotschevar – bewigged and perfumed, in fine robes, fingers ready with a pinch of snuff at all the right moments.

'Frau Frolich, were you employed as a housekeeper in the lodgings of Herr Ludwig van Beethoven?' Hotschevar asked.

'I was,' Frau Frolich replied timidly.

'How long were you in his employ?'

'For a month.'

'Only one month?' Hotschevar queried in mock surprise.

'Aye. No one could stand it longer than that.'

'I see. Please tell the court why.'

'The filth was bad enough. That man is mad. He can't hear a thing you say and he is always shouting and yelling. He stands naked as a jaybird in the mornings, bellowing like a singer in the opera, and pours water over his head, so much it drips to the floor below. The landlords are always half ready to chuck him out from his carryings on.'

'Was the boy, Karl, kept properly clean?' Hotschevar asked.

'He was filthy. Filthy as could be. His head was full of lice, and the master declared how it was so *very healthy* to have them,' replied Frau Frolich, heatedly.

'Was the uncle, Ludwig van Beethoven, able to adequately meet the needs of his charge?'

'The man cannot look after himself – not properly – much less a child.'

Schindler heard the words and wrote them down, sensing the impotent fury of Beethoven seated beside him. If ever he had the impression of being the messenger about to be murdered for the message he delivered, this was the moment. And it was not over yet. Lawyer Hotschevar, whose intellect was combined with a fine sense of drama, turned and called out to the magistrates, 'I would now like to call upon master Karl van Beethoven, son of Frau Johanna Beethoven, nephew to Ludwig van Beethoven.'

Schindler tried his best to restrain the master as he jumped to his feet, his face a mask of anger and confusion. He cried out, 'No! I forbid it! I *forbid* it!' He pulled away from Schindler, and set himself before the court. 'It is bad enough that *I* have to be exposed to the wretched and common gossip of these liars in the pay of that poisonous woman. But spare my poor nephew!'

The magistrates refused Beethoven's request, honoured composer though he might be, and who could blame them? With so many adults spreading unsubstantiated rumours, with the atmosphere rife with so much exaggeration and unbridled anger, why not trust to a fine, upstanding ten-year-old boy? And so Karl was called and took his place at the stand.

'Can you tell us how your Uncle treats you, Karl?' asked Hotschevar kindly. It was obvious that the young boy was terrified.

'Well,' came the response from Karl's small voice.

'He has a hot temper, does he not?'

'Yes.'

'Do you fear his temper?'

'No.'

'Has he ever punished you?'

'Only when I deserved it.'

'Karl, do you think your mother is a bad woman?'

Glancing across the courtroom, Schindler glimpsed Johanna, who looked on with rapt attention. Did he, Schindler, consider her a bad woman? He did not know.

Young Karl, for his part, did not answer.

Hotschevar decided to rephrase the question. 'Did your uncle repeatedly tell you that she was little better than a whore?'

'Yes.'

'And did you agree?'

'Only to make him happy,' replied Karl.

'So you lied ... Who would you prefer to live with? Your mother or your uncle? Do you want to stay with your uncle?'

'Yes.'

'Speak up.'

'Yes.' Karl's voice was louder but still shaky.

'You don't sound certain.'

'It would be better,' Karl said, 'if Uncle had someone to be with him, because he is hard of hearing and can't talk to me.'

'In fact,' Hotschevar interupted, 'he is stone deaf, isn't he?'

'Yes.'

'Karl, do you love your mother?'

'Yes.'

'Do you miss her?'

'Yes.'

'Then would you not prefer to live with her?'

Karl was silent. He averted his eyes and hung his head.

At this point Hotschevar turned to the magistrates. 'I submit to the court,' he pleaded, 'and I join with this deeply hurt mother, and with a quiet heart leave to the august judgement of this high and noble body the decision as to what it will see fit to decree in regard to the future education of this boy and the exercise of the guardianship over him. This in consideration of the fact that, as the foregoing makes plain, Herr Ludwig van Beethoven should be considered physically and morally *unfit* to have custody of this child and should therefore—'

'My uncle needs me,' Karl interrupted. 'What I would prefer is that we all live together.'

It was an unlikely outcome that the boy proposed, but any rational, sensible resolution seemed equally impossible. Beethoven had the upper hand in the legal battle until the Imperial Landrecht discovered by accident that he was not of noble birth. The magistrates presiding over the civil court for common people were more inclined to rule for Johanna. And so they did, returning Karl to her guardianship in 1819.

An infuriated Beethoven wrote letters and petitions all throughout the year. He used the messenger of his friend and piano pupil, the Archduke Rudolph, and asked for intervention on the part of Archduke Ludwig as well. The political influence of such powerful friends was obvious and enormous. To cap it all, Beethoven finally one day dragged Schindler off to see the Chancellor of Austria himself, Clemens Metternich.

Schindler tried to warn the master that this was not necessarily a good idea. It was true that Metternich was now the most powerful man in Europe. But the Karlsbad Decrees had just been put into effect the year before, and made a police state of Austria. Metternich had restored a stern literary censorship and had invested in secret police to root out all forms of subversive activity; he was determined to stamp out the very breath of change, much less revolution. And Beethoven, a former supporter of the French Revolution, was suspect. All the more because he was still inclined to vent his opinions in cafés and public places about the 'utter moral rottenness of the Austrian state'.

But the master, noted Schindler as they were ushered into the offices of the chancellor, had somewhere learned to bow deeply. And seated in the great high chairs passed down by the aristocracy to the bourgeoisie, beneath the gaze of Metternich in his book-lined study,

Beethoven was miraculously able to hold his tongue – almost.

Metternich opened gracefully. He said, 'Herr Beethoven, our most accomplished composer. It is an honour.'

Beethoven nodded, deaf and obliging.

Schindler spoke up, saying, 'Due to his infirmity, Herr Beethoven has requested that I speak for him.'

Metternich regarded Beethoven coolly. 'By all means.'

'His case in the magistracy is not going well. The wife of his dead brother, from whose deleterious care he hopes to remove his nephew, has bribed witnesses to testify against him.'

'My poor Karl!' Beethoven cut in loudly. 'He has been corrupted by her poisonous breath.'

'What Herr Beethoven means to say—' began Schindler.

'She is a plague to my Karl,' Beethoven interrupted, 'who had the misfortune to suck at his mother's breast.'

Schindler realized that the master was quickly losing control of himself. He gave him an alarmed glance, beseeching him to be calm.

Metternich watched impassively, fingering a police dossier, which he presently opened. As he gazed down at a page, he said, 'Tell me, Herr Beethoven. Why should I help you?'

Schindler braced himself. He had expected this. The Austrian police were extremely thorough about compiling their files on individuals. And Beethoven, known for his volubility, was a sure and easy target.

'"Metternich is a worse tyrant than Napoleon."' The chancellor raised his eyes briefly. 'That was recorded just last Tuesday at the Swan Tavern. "Metternich

should be forced to eat my shit." And so on. Herr
Beethoven, there are many forces in Austria that
foment revolt. I like lively discussion as much as the
next man, but I fear that these days we cannot allow
so much – how can I put it – enthusiasm. Perhaps it
would be better if our great artists were a little more
circumspect.'

The master, for once, bit his lip, realizing that he had
gone too far.

'Herr Beethoven,' spoke up Schindler, 'is an honorary
citizen of Vienna. He proposes to the chancellor that he
write a Grand Oratorio, praising all Austria and your
magnificent diplomacy at the Congress of Vienna,
which has secured peace for all Europe.'

Metternich smiled. It would not be a bad thing; in fact
it could be a bit of divine providence. He had been
abused by the cultural elite, and it was said that
nothing but dance tunes had been played at the Congress
of Vienna, orchestrated by the chancellor, five years
before. The Congress dances, it was said by wits, but
does not march forward.

'An Oratorio?' he asked.

'A Grand Oratorio,' said Schindler.

The Chancellor cocked his head in silent assent.

All of which led to that special and long-awaited day
before an appellate court, when the magistrates filed in
and took their places. The fact that Beethoven across
the courtroom appeared so superbly confident was not
lost upon Johanna. She felt a chill of anxiety.

'This court has seen fit,' declaimed the chief magistrate, 'to ordain that Johanna van Beethoven, the
widow of the late Caspar van Beethoven, shall be

completely excluded from the guardianship of her son, Karl van Beethoven. Henceforth, Ludwig van Beethoven is to be the sole guardian of this minor.'

Beethoven rose at the announcement of the verdict. He turned to smile at Karl and grasp the boy's shoulders. And Karl, now thirteen, appeared confused. He was certainly not happy.

On the other side of the courtroom, Jacob Hotschevar jumped to his feet. He shouted and stamped his feet at the magistrates, unable to control his disgust. 'This court is corrupt!' he roared.

Beethoven, so taken with himself at that moment – so wrapped up in savouring his victory – was smiling broadly. Johanna was suddenly within his line of vision, and she stared him down hard.

'I pray, Ludwig,' she said, 'that you will never suffer as I do.'

Although Beethoven could not hear her, what she said was plainly etched on her features. He turned quickly away from her gaze, bewildered. He looked at Schindler. His smile faltered.

Chapter 15

A Pyrrhic Victory

For Schindler, it was above all Beethoven the composer who suffered during the years of conflict over Karl. Instead of putting down notes and tones, the master was writing letters to the various courts and seeking the opinions and influence of people in high places – much of it useless verbiage in which he repeated, over and over, the same charges against Johanna.

'They were unedifying and regrettable testimonies to his inner agitation,' Schindler said to Anna Marie. 'In his passionate pursuit of Karl he lost all sense of balance.'

They had talked all morning, drunk endless cups of tea with bread and jam, and now, with the sky darkening in late afternoon as the sun dipped below the distant mountains, the innkeeper's daughter came by lighting candles. Still they continued to talk.

'Had I been there for him,' said Anna Marie, 'perhaps

I could have prevented this turn of events.' It struck Schindler that she was the first person he had spoken with who seemed to understand the enormity of Beethoven's misadventure.

During those years it was as though Beethoven and Johanna were locked in an embrace of mutual loathing; their conjugal bed was a court of law. Here was the most famous living composer of all Europe and the civilized world, with publishers grasping for his works in Paris, London, and Leipzig as well as Vienna – and what was he writing? A long correspondence with a hausfrou about the way to run a household, all in anticipation of bringing Karl to live with him under conditions approved by the court. *How often are servants to be given roast meat? Do maids get the same meat as the master? How many pounds is enough for three people? How much bread money for the housekeeper and cook per day?* Beethoven was astonished that a roll a day for the kitchenmaid could come to eighteen florins a year. The hausfrau had to fight the master for every kreuzer to buy milk and butter and was constantly under suspicion of cheating. He opened the eggs himself – Schindler found this both poetic and disgraceful – and if they were less than perfectly fresh, he would throw them at the cook.

He never admitted to his petty tyranny, nor did he seem aware of the larger problem. After the death of Caspar and the fight for Karl began, Beethoven's musical output slowed to a trickle – a tragic outcome, Schindler thought, for mankind present and future. In five years he wrote only one sonata, and one cantata for Prince Lobkowitz' birthday in 1816. He began but did not finish either the Oratorio he promised Metternich

172

or the Mass he contracted for with the London Philharmonic. Nor was there another symphony after the Eighth, in 1814.

'There were rumours that he was finished, is it not so?' asked the countess.

'Yes,' said Schindler. 'In Vienna the word was that he was written out. His deafness had worsened and everyone thought it had finished him. Meanwhile Rossini had come to town and performed *The Thieving Magpie*. Italian Opera was all the rage. The great and profound works of Beethoven were seldom performed, his music no longer current – a scandal in itself.'

'But they were wrong,' said the countess with a sad smile. 'That is a consolation.'

'Yes,' said Schindler. 'After the court suit was settled, he began to write again, and it was magnificent. It is a measure of his genius.'

But even after he resumed work and put in long hours on music instead of nonsense, Beethoven's spiritual isolation, through much of the third decade of the nineteenth century, only deepened. It showed profoundly in the master's appearance, his manners, his way of life, his unique way of being in the world. Metternich's secret police had no trouble keeping track of his opinions, because he gave them out so very loudly in cafés, in sudden, angry outbursts. '*Austrians, Austrians*,' he would shout, heedless of the consequences. '*The Viennese are worthless from the Emperor down.*' In the proper context of low comedy, his outbursts could have been charming. But delivered with such virulence, and with police spies everywhere, they were not only tactless but dangerous.

He moved constantly, from one apartment to the next.

He enraged his landlords with his disorderly ways, and by talking and singing to himself at the top of his lungs and constantly calling for water in which to bathe. And he was forever haranguing them over some detail in the housekeeping, or some untoward remark on their part or imagined slight. It became a common sight in the streets of Vienna to see a cart loaded with Beethoven's belongings – including his two pianos and all his sketches and composition books – on the way to new rooms. And although he hated moving, no sooner did he land somewhere than he was ready, at the slightest provocation, to run all over the city looking for something else.

Physically Beethoven aged a great deal during these years as his health, always fragile, began to deteriorate; and his physical decline was accompanied by more and more frequent bouts of rage. He suffered from jaundice, exacerbated by his heavy intake of wine, and occasionally he bent double with intestinal pain. His head was now covered with long, bushy, grey hair. Although he still had his penetrating gaze, he walked the streets head down, wielding a cane, the collar of his long overcoat turned up, his hands clasped behind his back, oblivious to the hearing world, gesticulating to himself.

'Sometimes street urchins would mock him and throw stones,' said Schindler, shaking his head. 'They ran after him as if he were an old lunatic.'

And not only street urchins. One night he wandered into the suburbs and was arrested in the Wiener Neustadt for peering into windows and for vagrancy. The police threw him in the cell with the town drunks and derelicts, and he howled, *I am Ludwig van Beethoven!'* Which amused his cell companions, who, in the general hilarity and to humour this madman who called himself the great Beethoven, included Napoleon and Shakespeare and Jesus Christ among their numbers. But he repeated his claim so often and so loudly that something had to be done. He insisted that the town's musical director be summoned. In due course Herr Herzog was waken up, in the middle of the night, and came down to the jail.

'This *is* Beethoven!' he cried, shocked. He took the master home, gave him a clean bed and fresh linen. In the morning the master was sent back to Vienna in the magisterial coach, with apologies from the Burgomaster.

'This was his victory,' said Schindler, sadly.

'And he had Karl,' said Anna Marie.

'Lord help us,' said Schindler, nodding and remembering, not with any pleasure.

Beethoven's 'trouser button', Karl, had been a nice young lad at nine, when his father Caspar died. He was not unhappy to form a paternal relationship with his uncle Ludwig, whom he knew was a famous man. But he loved his mother. When he was put in private school, he took every opportunity to see her. He did not understand what it meant that his mother was a harlot, and when he was prevented from seeing his mother, he ran away to her, or stumbled in his studies, or made himself unbearable in one way or another. It was bad enough when he attended boarding school, but when he and his uncle came to inhabit the same rooms together, it was a recipe for disaster.

I cannot eat until I have finished crying; it would be poison if I tried to eat in this state of vexation.

Now I see that out of dislike, you will not even bestow a look on me. I thought I could speak what I think. But in the future I shall be careful not even to say that, if I see that it hurts you.

Schindler regularly came across Karl's whimperings and reproaches in the Conversation Books, usually on the morning after a night of quarrelling. Although their fights weighed lightly on Beethoven – he would move quickly from rage to remorse to utter forgetfulness – Karl did not so easily forget or forgive. The boy had become a teenager with a teenager's unsettled nerves and moodiness. Although the five years of struggle over his fate had robbed his nature of its inherent sweetness, he was still reasonably good most of the time, and worked hard at school – still proud, even with their problems, to be Beethoven's nephew.

But at the age of fourteen Karl was not allowed to choose his pursuits normally. It was at this age that Beethoven decided, against all his own precepts, that the boy would be taught the piano; he even nurtured fantasies that Karl was destined to be a great virtuoso.

'It never occurred to the master,' said Schindler, 'that he was trying to do for Karl what his own father had tried to do for him. And of course the results were tragic.'

'Yes, tragic,' said Anna Marie.

'He sent him to Czerny,' said Schindler. 'Czerny himself had once studied under the master, and his pupils have included Franz Liszt and the Princess of Wales.' Schindler frowned, recalling the sequence of events. 'But there was nothing he could do for Karl. The talent simply wasn't there.'

'So Beethoven taught Karl himself?' asked the countess.

'Yes – and with a vengeance. He had Karl do endless scales and *arpeggios*. The boy was completely without touch or flair, and could scarcely keep time. But the master would stand behind him as he played, and watch his hands – for although he could not hear, he could see every mistake. But he was determined to make a virtuoso of Karl against all the odds. Nothing was going to stand in his way.'

Karl, who had started to lose weight and to suffer from insomnia, was beside himself when he found the draft of a notice that Beethoven intended to send to the printer. He brought it to Schindler and handed it to him without a word.

The Maestro Ludwig van Beethoven takes pleasure in announcing a concert which shall consist in the debut of his nephew and stepchild Karl van Beethoven, a prodigy taught and instructed by the Maestro himself.

Schindler read the note, a little amused – Karl was then seventeen, far too old to qualify as a prodigy – but also concerned. He said, carefully, 'Why, this is wonderful. The very thing to raise his spirits. You must be very excited.'

Karl stared at him. 'Anton, have you ever heard me play?'

'Not recently,' said Schindler.

'You have to help me,' Karl said. 'I'm in a terrible state of mind. He barely lets me out of his sight. If I go anywhere there are always angry reproaches when I return. He waits for me outside the school gates. Imagine the ridicule of my classmates. I am seventeen

177

years old, but he wants to lead me home by the hand. I have no companions, he doesn't allow it. He constantly loads me down with errands so that it's impossible for me to study. I am compelled to spend endless hours at the keyboard. For what? *For what?*' Karl laughed bitterly. 'He can't hear my ham-fisted playing. And he does no work himself. All he does is scribble incomprehensible phrases. Or bellows them at the top of his lungs. A stupid childish tune. He says this is the motif for a grand symphony. Ridiculous!'

Karl then hummed a few bars from what – Schindler later recognized – became the Ode to Joy, the Chorale which formed part of the Ninth Symphony. But even Schindler could make no sense at the time of what sounded like musical doggerel.

'I think he's going mad,' said Karl. 'You must help me. I'm desperate.'

With Schindler's guidance, Karl composed a note which together they presented to Beethoven. It pleaded with the master to forestall plans for the concert. It also tried, with subtle indirection, to give him a sense of proportion about Karl's modest gifts. Beethoven read the note with growing agitation.

'So I am to abandon my plans, eh? I am placing *intolerable pressure* on Karl. He is a *mediocre* talent.'

They both put down their responses in the Conversation Book.

'*Someone must tell you, master,*' said Schindler simply. '*The boy is a mediocre talent.*'

'*What Anton says is true,*' Karl wrote in the Book after Schindler.

'Karl,' said Beethoven sourly, 'don't you realize there are always asinine fellows like this Schindler, with

178

their commonplace opinions that come from their commonplace minds? I have suffered enough of them in my day.'

'*Anton is right*,' wrote Karl. '*I am a plumber on the piano.*'

'Oh, so Anton Schindler knows more about music than Ludwig van Beethoven.'

'*This is too much*,' wrote Schindler. '*You must stop torturing the boy!*'

'Schindler,' said Beethoven, 'I always found you a bore and an ass but you had your uses. Now you have none. You have outlived your usefulness to me. Get out.'

'And in fact, for a time – until that tragic day when Karl tried to take his life – I saw less of Beethoven,' Schindler told the countess.

'We have all had such contretemps with him,' said Anna Marie.

'The violinist Holz took my place in the master's affections. And he could in some ways do more.'

Holz, for example, was willing to spy on Karl; he accompanied him everywhere, pretended to be his friend, and informed on his every move to Beethoven.

When Karl turned eighteen, his arguments with Beethoven grew more bitter; almost every subject they touched on led to an explosion. Karl had wanted a military career from the time he was very young, but Beethoven insisted that if he couldn't be a pianist, he must study philology. Always obedient, even when his heart was adamantly opposed, Karl was assiduous in his studies, but he could not make up in industry for lack of feeling and talent for the subject. When he failed the course, Beethoven accused him of laziness. But they saved their worst quarrels for the shades and nuances surrounding the issue of Karl's growing interest in women.

'I hate to speak about this,' said Schindler, 'and I frankly find it embarrassing.'

'You mean that he was overly concerned about the boy's virginity?' said the countess.

'Yes.'

'Virginity,' said the countess, smiling, 'is a losing battle in Vienna.'

As with both Caspar and Johann, so with Karl – sexual jealousy and suspicion on Beethoven's part brought them to violent confrontation. Beethoven constantly warned Karl to stay away from the 'fortresses' as he called prostitutes, and he lectured him on the dangers of venereal disease, which he referred to quaintly as 'poisonous breath from dragons'. This obsession with the boy's sexuality only worsened their relationship as Karl muddled his way through adolescence.

In the summer of 1824, when Karl refused to go with Beethoven to Baden, the master was concerned that he was bedding every wench in Vienna. He wrote to his nephew daily on the virtues of celibacy before marriage – a practice he had never permitted himself – and then defended himself by saying: *Do not think I have anything but your well-being and welfare in mind.* Once back Vienna, with Karl under his wing, there was the wrenching problem of the servants.

'He had begun to treat them with great unfairness,' said Schindler. 'But with Karl his suspicions reached an alarming degree and became a self-fulfilling prophecy.'

Seldom did a housekeeper remain in Beethoven's service more than a few weeks. One was the 'Old Witch', the next the 'Old Devil', and then the 'Old Biddy' and 'Satan' and 'Wild Animal' and the 'Old Goose' and 'Vulgar Kitchen Creature'. They were all somewhat up in years, and not likely to attract a libidinous young man.

But then there was Nanette.

Perhaps Beethoven had hired her as a Temptress; Schindler did not know. But the same wrenching scene was repeated with her as with all the rest. One evening, pretty, curvaceous, raven-haired Nanette brought the roast beef with sauce to the table.

'It's late,' said Beethoven sourly.

'I'm sorry, sir.'

'And disgusting.' Beethoven pushed away the plate. 'I told you what meat to buy. Why do you disobey me? My bowels are in a terrible state. You are poisoning me.'

Karl could not stand such comments. For years he had objected to them. He wrote in the book, *'Why are you torturing her?'*

'She may appear plump and pretty but she is a vulgar bitch,' said Beethoven. 'She gossips and laughs about me all over town.'

'You know that is not true,' wrote Karl. *'Why say such terrible things?'*

'Are you siding with that kitchen creature against me?'

'I am merely saying that she has done no wrong,' wrote Karl. *'She works hard.'*

'On you, perhaps,' said Beethoven with a sneer. He called the girl back. 'Your food is poison. You are fired.'

Nanette burst into sobs and, after a quick glance at Karl, fled from the room.

181

Karl could stand no more. His face dark with anger, his heart beating wildly, he rose to go after the girl as Beethoven shouted, 'Wait!' and brandished the Conversation Book. 'Write.'

'You foul old bastard!' Karl shouted at him.

'You are evil, just like your mother!' Beethoven screamed in return. 'Leave me then. Leave me here with nothing to eat. After all I've done for you. After all the sacrifices!'

Karl left the room without another word, slamming the door behind him. When he did not return within a few hours, Beethoven donned his grey overcoat and his hat, and he went out searching. He passed old friends, who stopped him, and he told them, 'My Karl has gone. Have you seen him? He is not worth finding, but what is a father to do?'

He was certain that Karl was with Nanette. He was certain the boy had been sleeping with her. In Beethoven's fevered imagination she had become a sort of incarnation of evil, a succubus, a devil in skirts.

He entered the tavern, which was filled not only with students but with low persons of every stripe. He pushed his way through the crush of drunks to the back, where prostitutes flirted on the laps of young men. He asked the barman, 'Have you seen my Karl?'

The barman could not write an answer, which complicated matters. Beethoven appealed to his neighbours, and grew more frustrated with every laugh and shrug. A glass of wine appeared in front of him, and he downed it helplessly in a single swallow.

Then he spotted Karl.

He was with Nanette, his arm draped over her shoulder, his hand cupping the underside of her breast, a glass of beer at his lips. He was whispering in her ear and laughing. Muttering under his breath, Beethoven strode over to Karl and wrenched the stein out of his hand, spraying him with beer. *'Come with me,'* he shouted.

He grabbed hold of Karl and, with a surprising show of strength, dragged the boy out of his chair. When Nanette tried to force her way between them, Beethoven slapped her with an open hand and sent her reeling.

'Whore! Begone!' he shouted.

As patrons stopped their conversations to watch the action, more amused than concerned, Beethoven took his nephew by the hair and dragged him through the tavern and out into the street. There Karl, screaming and crying, broke his uncle's grip and began to run away. Beethoven started after him but suddenly doubled over in pain, spiked by his disintegrating liver. He collapsed to the street. From a safe distance, Karl thought at first it was a joke, just another cruel form of blackmail. But when the old fool went into a paroxysm of coughing, he returned to stand over him.

'Uncle,' he said, leaning over him, 'why do you treat me this way? Why can't I live my life?'

He helped Beethoven to his feet, hired a cab, and took him home.

'And after that episode,' said Schindler, 'I understand that Karl was not the same. He slipped into an unhappy period where he was always miserable. He failed in his philology and took a commercial course. But when the exams came around, he was going to fail that as well.'

'What he did next hurt Beethoven most of all,' said the

countess. 'I still remember that as though it were yesterday.'

'Yes,' said Schindler. 'Karl gave expression to his anger in a way that caused the master a mortal wound.'

Chapter 16

On a Summer's Day

'What Karl did, exactly, has been determined by the authorities,' said Schindler. 'His intentions, broadly speaking, he had made clear for some days.'

Beethoven had not gone to the countryside in the summer of 1826, ostensibly because of ill health. But the real reason was Karl. With examinations approaching, Karl remained in Vienna to study with his crammer. Beethoven was hesitant to leave him, afraid that the boy would go whoring, gambling, or – even worse – insist on seeing his mother.

Controlling Karl was becoming increasingly difficult. Because they could no longer live under the same roof with any kind of harmony, Beethoven had paid for Karl's lodging with Herr Schlemmer – though the boy's presence was required in the evenings. Schlemmer kept close tabs on the boy, at Beethoven's request, and one day in late July he found a loaded pistol, together with lead and powder, in Karl's clothing chest. Frau

Schlemmer found its mate in a drawer. Neither Herr Schlemmer nor his wife had the slightest familiarity with guns, and had to ask a neighbour to unload them. They wasted no time reporting their news to Beethoven.

'Be lenient with him,' urged Herr Schlemmer, who was familiar with Beethoven's temper, 'or he will despair.'

Holz – who Beethoven still preferred at that period to Schindler – bungled his mission to retrieve Karl when he found him at school.

Karl told Holz, 'What good would it do to stop me? If I don't escape today, I shall do so later.' And then he fled.

'I have no idea how inwardly determined he was,' said Schindler to the countess. 'I only know what he did.'

'It was all so romantic, in a way,' said Anna Marie. 'The castle ruins of Rauhenstein. Romantic and tragic at the same time.'

'We are all romantics in Vienna,' said Schindler seriously. 'And there were other pressing problems. He had some gambling debts, and he had filched some of Beethoven's books to sell. His exams were approaching, and he was sure to fail them, even with the help of his crammer.'

'But that was not the real reason,' she said. 'It was the master. And his mother.'

Schindler shook his head neutrally. 'We can only speculate.'

This much was certain: Karl pawned his gold watch and chain, and with the few florins he received, he purchased another pair of duelling pistols. They were smooth-bore flintlocks with nine-inch barrels and elaborate scroll work. He also bought balls and powder. Karl then walked to the Kartener Gate, where he boarded the mail coach to Baden.

That it was a warm Saturday in July, Schindler remembered well. He was asleep, although fitfully, an hour before dawn, when he heard a loud banging from outside his window, and then someone shouting his name. He awoke, threw open the sash and peered out to see Beethoven, turning around and around in circles in the street, and beating his walking stick against the chassis of the carriage. Schindler rubbed his eyes, but it was no dream.

'Wake up, you bastard!' cried Beethoven. And added, with an irony more pitiful than amusing: 'He has gone. Gone! And it is *all your fault*, Schindler.'

Karl, meanwhile, spent the night in Baden, which was then in the midst of the holiday season. The next morning he stopped down in the tavern of the inn and ordered a brandy for breakfast. Drinking at any and all hours was not uncommon in those parts, and the barman thought nothing of it. Even so, he sensed that something was not right when, at ten o'clock, while church bells rang, Karl staggered out after having drunk several brandies.

He carried the gun case quite openly – target practice was a common sport in Baden – and, just as carefree as a Sunday painter with his palette and oils, he mounted the castle ruins of Rauhenstein. It was an exceptional morning in the Helenenthal. Tall, thick trees beneath wisps of clouds sailing in a clear blue sky greeted him as he arrived at the summit of the cliff. Squirrels stopped nibbling to watch him, birds let out a chatter, midges danced in the sunlight. Karl opened the case and took out one of the revolvers and some ammunition.

'*I embrace you lovingly*,' his uncle Ludwig had written to him a few days before, after one of their ghastly scenes, '*and am convinced that soon you will no longer misunderstand me, thus I judge your conduct . . .*'

Karl did understand him. And he felt that perhaps when his uncle found his body, he would realize as much. What he was about to do was not something a little boy does. He was not a little boy, even though his uncle still insisted on picking him up from school and walking home with him arm in arm when he was nearly twenty.

I am not as frivolous as you believe.

So Karl had written to Beethoven just the day before yesterday, when he was offered a familiar litany of insults and derogatory remarks. And perhaps, Schindler thought, he intended to show his uncle that he was serious, even though he had failed at philology and at commercial studies, and was likely to fail at anything else he undertook. He was *serious*, even though he wanted to leave the house from time to time without a chaperon, and could not bear to pass every evening with his uncle, playing piano solos for four hands and arguing over trifles. *Serious*, even with a few gambling debts.

And he had hardly been guilty of misappropriating the eighty florins due Schlemmer for the rent in May. He truly did not know what had happened to the receipt. And as for the books . . .

The bedlam of your rooms is so great, he wrote to Beethoven, *that it is not to be believed. You accuse me of stealing eighty florins because you cannot find the receipt. But when you lost the manuscript for the Kyrie of the Missa Solemnis, where did we find it? It was used to wrap the butter!*

'All these reproaches were to come to an end,' said Schindler. 'There on the mountaintop. He was serious. He would not fail this time.'

'Yes, he had a sonata of his own,' said the countess.

'And not used to wrap butter,' said Schindler, 'but gunpowder.'

Karl tore open the small paper packet with his teeth and dumped the powder down the muzzle, followed by the ball, which he drove home with the rod. He followed the same procedure with the other pistol, probably because he doubted that should the first shot misfire or should his aim be off, he would have the nerve to load again.

Then it became merely a question of inching towards the edge of the cliff, holding the pistol to his temple and firing. Karl took one last look at the majesty of Aquae Panoniae, with its gorgeous girth of mountains, and perhaps he asked himself if his life had become truly intolerable and unacceptable. Whatever his response, he felt the muzzle of the gun touch his forehead. He pulled the trigger.

The sharp report of the pistol's fire shattered the quiet on the ruins of Rauhenstein. Squirrels flung down their nuts and ran for cover and birds grew briefly quiet. Instead of falling off the cliff, Karl was blown back by the blast and lost his balance. When he hit the ground he felt blood pouring down his face, but he did not lose consciousness. He must have sensed right then that he had failed once again. The ball had not lodged in his skull, it was clear to him, but must have skimmed the surface. His brain was not laid open, or else he would not be feeling this terrible pain; he would be feeling nothing; he would *be* nothing. The world, and all of its problems, would have vanished forever.

There remained the second revolver, if only he could locate it. His head throbbed horribly, and he could not help crying out in pain, but at the same time, he glimpsed through tears and blood the other pistol. He raised this firearm to his temple, as he had the first. Although he congratulated himself on his good sense in loading the second, he had not counted on another factor – that he no longer could count on a steady hand.

'Nevertheless,' said Schindler, with bitter sarcasm, 'one must try. Because one is young and one is foolish. And thinks only of one's self.'

So Karl pulled the trigger and the second bullet left the muzzle and entered his skull.

'A passing carter found him,' Schindler told the countess. 'He was not dead. Karl asked to be taken to Johanna's. It was there that we found him.'

Johanna responded to Beethoven's hammering on the door of her house. She opened it partway, glanced at Beethoven and Schindler with terrified, unseeing eyes, but attempted to bar their way inside.

'Stand aside!' cried Beethoven. 'I know you have him.'

'My Karl has shot himself.'

'*Stand aside!*'

Beethoven had heard nothing of what she said, and Schindler was obliged to write it down for him. *Karl has attempted suicide.* When he showed him the slate, Beethoven collapsed. It was some moments before smelling salts were brought and he was revived. Johanna was hysterical. She kept telling Schindler, 'I beg you, ask the surgeon not to make a report. They will arrest him. Suicide is a crime.'

'We must call the surgeon,' said Schindler.

Karl was still in shock when they entered the room, shivering and sometimes twitching, surely frightened by what he had done to himself, and there was blood on the pillow and a bowl of water and towels on the night stand. Johanna had apparently been bathing his wounds. But as Schindler looked, it seemed that much of what seemed to be a horrible wound was only blackened blood.

'I have been waiting for you, Uncle,' said Karl. A strange, fractured smile spread across his pale-white, blood-spattered features. 'Give me the book.'

Beethoven was speechless, unable to move, as he studied his nephew. Schindler gave Karl the notebook, and the young man, grinning all the while, wrote a brief line with trembling hand.

'Never show your face to me again.'

Karl did not die. The first bullet had grazed his skull; the second, though it lodged in his skull, did not penetrate it and was easily operable. The fear was that an infection might develop, and so Karl was transferred to the care of surgeons at the general hospital in Vienna, where he remained for six weeks. The surgeons wasted no time in bringing his case to the attention of the police. An investigation was launched, for suicide was indeed a crime in Austria. Karl was suspected of harbouring anti-religious sentiments and, while in the hospital, was forced to take church instruction. A strict

Redemptionist came every day and stuck to him like a leech until he was satisfied that Karl was not fundamentally a sinner and had a good Christian attitude. When the police asked Karl why he had attempted to kill himself, he gave an answer in no uncertain terms.

'Because my uncle harassed me so. I felt I was going mad.'

'His cruelty towards the master, his saying what he said to the authorities, forever changed my opinion of Karl,' admitted Schindler to the countess. 'It may not be just of me. But if I admit the truth, I have never again been able to countenance the sight of him.'

In the days after Karl's attempted suicide, Beethoven alternated between wrath, exasperation and confusion. He could accept no conscious responsibility for what the boy had done, and wrote that in his opinion it was all due to: *Confusion of mind and insanity and heat. He was afflicted with headaches from childhood.* He complained to Schindler that he did not even want to visit Karl at the hospital; and when he went, as of course he did, he dressed and acted like a ragamuffin. And as he sat beside the boy's bed, he soon grew angry – Schindler could scarcely blame him – and commenced his usual reproaches against Johanna, calling her once more Queen of the Night.

Karl listened grimly and then wrote: *'I want to hear nothing about her that is derogatory, and it is absolutely not my place to pass judgement on her.'*

It was as though a new Karl had been born from the old.

'And perhaps it was only fair of Karl to say that,' added Schindler. 'He had put up with so many assaults from the master over the years. But for all that, I now quite detest the boy. His heart was not large enough to grasp Beethoven's love for him.'

Schindler's loyalty and his own heart were, as ever, with the master, and anything that dimnished him was unacceptable. To criticize the master, to be angry or even enraged with him, he understood. He knew the cost of being associated with genius. But Karl's suicide attempt struck at the master's deepest recesses of being. It was a way of murdering the master's soul, and Schindler could not accept it. Beethoven had aged twenty years in the moments after his nephew's suicide attempt, and in the months that followed it became clear that it had shattered him in both mind and body. In a sense, it led to his death.

'It was decided that Karl would enter the army,' said Schindler, 'as he had always wanted to do in any event. A commission was obtained for him with Field Marshal Stutterheim for his regiment in Iglau. I must confess I was ecstatic. It would get Karl out of Vienna.'

It was in principle a great relief for everyone. Beethoven, relieved at the solution, dedicated his magnificent new string quartet in C sharp minor to Stutterheim.

'This was near the end,' said the countess.

'Yes,' said Schindler, nodding sadly.

It was only necessary for Karl to wait for his commission until his hair grew long enough to conceal the scars. In the meantime, his Uncle Johann invited Karl and Beethoven to stay with him and his wife, Therese, at their home in Gneixendorf. Schindler applauded this arrangement because it would simplify Karl's transition out of Beethoven's life. But when the hair took its own good time at growing, tensions began to grow in the family circle. Johann asked Ludwig to pay a little bed and board, to which the master objected. He also felt that Johann's wife Therese, a fine-looking buxom woman, was playing too much piano with Karl, and suspected a liaison. Karl himself fell into sullen moods. For a time, the family cease-fire held in place, but was broken towards the end of November, 1826, by a violent argument between the brothers. It was time to go.

On the return trip to Vienna, on a cold and rainy night in a wet December, Beethoven caught a chill. He and Karl travelled in an open carriage, and stayed one night at an inn whose accommodations were primitive, with no fireplace, and not even shutters on the windows. By the time they crossed the Danube and passed through the Struber Gate, the master had developed, in addition to dropsy, the first symptoms of a severe inflammation of the lungs, which occasioned the illness that would be his last.

Chapter 17

The Identity of the Immortal Beloved, Revealed

Now they had come full circle. Anna Marie had compelled Schindler to recount the master's story nearly to his deathbed. They had talked through yet another day and night, and dawn was breaking, and still Schindler was in no state to rest. They had spoken at such length, with Beethoven between them as a shared object of affection, that a strong bond had grown between them.

And the Immortal Beloved?

'Do you now know who she is?' the countess asked, resting her hand on Schindler's.

'But it cannot be...' He shook his head. He knew, and yet did not want to know, was not quite ready to accept the truth. 'I have been a fool.'

'You cannot blame yourself.'

'But I do blame myself, just as he blamed himself. And now that he's gone, how can we be reconciled?' He indicated the letter on the table between them. 'By that, I hope. I must deliver it to her.'

'In those last years,' said Anna Marie, 'I was not in Vienna.'

'I remember,' said Schindler.

'I, too, paid Metternich a visit, though not of my own free will. I was accused of being a political subversive. My intimacy with Ludwig was brought up, as though it were an embarrassment to my husband, the count, whom I had not seen in years. I was exiled – and Metternich was aware that Beethoven was bound by an agreement to stay in Vienna.' She sighed. 'Ironically, which I myself had put into effect.'

Schindler nodded. The countess had initiated the annuity which was Beethoven's provided he remained in Vienna. And Schindler recalled Beethoven's agitation at the forced departure of the countess; it was just at the time of all his machinations to retain custody of Karl.

'He brought Karl with him to Jedlersee in the summer of 1817,' said the countess. 'It was a wonderful, delightful interlude for us. Perhaps the best, most untroubled time we ever had together. Ludwig played with the children in the garden, he pretended to be a bear and let them chase him.' Anna Marie paused and remembered, a slight smile playing on her lips but with sadness in her eyes. 'Then,' she continued slowly, 'one day he took my hand. And I knew what he was going to say...' She paused again, forcing away tears. 'He took my hand with much tenderness, and he asked whether Karl might not in some measure replace August, the son I had lost. It was, or should have been, a beautiful moment, but I felt shadows, strange shadows, all around me. I said to him, "It is terrible to lose a son. I know the sorrow that Johanna must feel." Ludwig's tenderness then vanished in a second. He flushed in anger and raged, *"She has no right to him!"*

'I said, "But she is his mother."

'It was, for a time, over between us after that. Ludwig stormed back to Vienna. I did not receive an apology for months.'

'But he did apologize to you,' said Schindler. 'It was rare for the master to allow himself what he considered a weakness.'

'I would have suffered his temper. I would have suffered his moods. I would have given them both a home.' The countess shook her head. 'But life in Vienna had become no better than the war.'

'It was Metternich.'

'Beethoven and I renewed our love,' the countess continued. 'We fought. We reconciled. We lived like a family; there were hopes for a future together. And I can tell you this – this about your Immortal Beloved . . .' Her voice trembled now as she forced out the words; words that came with difficulty as she recalled once more that scene from long ago.

She awoke one night to discover that Beethoven had left her bed. She felt an odd sensation, a vague, sudden fear, and went searching for him. She found him seated before the doors which opened to the garden, gazing up at a star-filled sky.

'I approached him and put my arms around his shoulders. A letter was in his hand. When he turned to me, I could read some of the words.' She picked up the letter from the table, and said, 'These were the words:

"Why this deep grief when necessity speaks? Can our love subsist, except by sacrifices, by not asking everything? Can you change the fact that you are not wholly mine—I am not wholly yours? Oh, Lord, gaze at beautiful nature and resign yourself to what must be. Love demands everything and rightly so; and thus it is for me with you and for you with me."'

Anna Marie looked up at Beethoven then, her heart aching with love for him. His eyes stared back at her filled with an unrequited need. For the briefest of moments she believed the letter was addressed to her, until he said with bitter sarcasm, 'Is that not a noble and deep declaration of love?'

'Ludwig...' Something was not right; she felt a shattering inside of her.

Beethoven went on, oblivious to her, caught in the past. He said, 'I found it discarded in her room. Tossed aside under some dirty dishes. The letter meant nothing.'

And that was when Anna Marie realized the letter had been written to someone else, was meant for another.

'I risked everything,' Beethoven said, his voice husky with emotion, 'and she betrayed me. I opened my heart to her and she betrayed me.'

The countess now regarded Schindler with an expression deeper than regret, deeper than sadness. She said, 'It was she who came between us. I loved him completely, but he could never return my feelings for him. Because he could never forget her. After all those years she still lived inside of him.'

Schindler shook his head. 'I failed him.'

'We all failed him,' said Anna Marie.

'He gave us so much and we could not even make his existence tolerable. This one last wish must be as he wanted. He left her his estate. Tell me now. Tell me her name.'

'But you know, Herr Schindler.'

He lowered his head. 'It's so outrageous. It cannot be.'

'But it is. As a man of the world you must understand there is no logic in these matters.' She dipped a pen in ink and slowly wrote the name of the Immortal Beloved so that he could see it in black and white. He stared at the name.

'It cannot be,' he repeated.

The countess nodded. 'The answer was always in front of you. You just didn't want to see.'

Chapter 18

The Last Symphony

Schindler, once he was certain of her identity, decided to return to Vienna immediately. He ordered his bags brought down before breakfast was served, and Anna Marie saw him off.

As he entered the carriage, and reached out his arm to her, she surprised him with a kiss on the lips.

'Go to her.'

Schindler nodded. 'It's my duty.'

Anna Marie smiled up at him. 'You will please the master. He would have wanted this. Perhaps, after all, he was right when he said that he could not live without her.'

I can live only completely with you or not at all. Yes, it must be.

She was not in Vienna, as it turned out. Schindler located her with the help of Jacob Hotschevar, who greeted him with a lawyer's cordial reticence. Did he wish to see Frau Beethoven? It might be arranged. She lived in Baden. He could contact her and if the lady in question wished, a meeting might be arranged.

'I will go to Baden myself,' said Schindler. 'I have important news for her.'

'About her son?'

'Herr Hotschevar,' Schindler said stiffly, 'this is a matter between her and me.'

'She may need legal counsel,' said Hotschevar, and added through pursed lips, 'does it involve Beethoven?'

Schindler could barely control his impatience. 'If Frau Beethoven feels the need for counsel, I'm certain she will call on you.' He tipped his hat. 'Good day.'

Despite a certain anxiety, Schindler was confident, almost buoyant, as he approached Johanna's upholstery shop in Baden. The place was crowded with settees and love seats and lounges and chairs in various states of completion; Johanna was working on one which was particularly ornate, hammering fabric into place. The appearance of Schindler must have seemed like an apparition from the past. She looked startled and Schindler watched her features stiffen; she visibly steeled herself.

He bowed. He knew that he was not good with women like Johanna, who were more physical than ethereal beings; he did not feel comfortable around them and always stumbled for words. He tried to put extra warmth in his voice as he said, 'Frau Beethoven. May we speak in private?'

'I have nothing to hide from my employees.'

'Please. I implore you.'

She stared at him, her face a cool mask, and then said slowly, 'We can talk in the store room.'

Johanna sat nervously on the front few inches of a half-finished couch, Schindler on a packing case.

'A nice place you have here,' Schindler said. 'It's very much as the master once described it to me.'

'As you can see, I am very busy,' she said impatiently, interrupting his attempt at small talk. 'What brings you to Baden?'

'Yes, of course.' Schindler cleared his throat. 'Frau Beethoven, there's no easy way into this. May I see a sample of your handwriting?'

'What? But why?'

'Please. Indulge me. Your signature, for example. Anything written in script.'

'This is ridiculous.'

'Please, Frau Beethoven. I will explain in a moment.'

Sucking in her lips in agitation, she withdrew from the pocket of her apron a bill of sale and handed it to him. He compared it with the page from the registry of the Swan hotel in Karlsbad. Was it the same? He squinted, studying it. It looked the same, the same scrawls and loops, but he couldn't be entirely certain. He handed her the registry.

'Is this your handwriting?' he said.

'This can't be deciphered,' she said, puzzled. 'What is this?'

Schindler said, 'It is a page from the registry of the Swan Hotel in Karlsbad.'

She stared at him, her mouth open, shock written on her face. Then she looked again at the page from the registry. As she stood up to reply, her voice faltered.

'Frau Beethoven, did you write this?' he said gently.

'I would like you to go,' she said.

'I can't overestimate the importance of your answers. Did you ever meet Beethoven in Karlsbad?'

'What? What are you saying to me?'

'Did you?'

She gathered her wits about her, and he could see the effort of will it took. 'You can hardly be unaware of the manner in which I suffered at his hands, Herr Schindler. I find the question as insulting as it is impudent. What are you implying?'

He shook his head. 'There can be no peace without the truth.' Their eyes met and held.

'For you perhaps,' she said at last. After a moment she added: 'I have made my peace with Ludwig.'

'You wanted nothing to do with him after the lawsuit was settled in his favour,' said Schindler. 'I remember that.'

'I have made my peace,' she repeated.

She then told Schindler when and where she and Beethoven had seen each other for the last time.

'Even though I had hated him for so long, even though he had tried to destroy me, I went. I had to go. I knew it was his swan song.'

It was the opening performance, at the Karntnerthor, of Beethoven's last and greatest symphony, the Ninth. He had ceased work upon it while he battled Johanna, and took it up again only much later. Its grandeur drew from its mingling of darkness and light, of death and life, of the triumph of joy, brotherhood and benevolence. Dramatic notes and tones echoed throughout the symphony, exploding the boundaries of the musical form and bringing to life the longing of humanity for freedom, for joy and for love.

Johanna pressed her way into the Karntnerthor slightly late, and at first could not see him. She wondered if some last minute slight had sent him into a fit of rage and caused him to walk out. But in a moment nothing mattered except the music. 'I was totally captured by it,' she told Schindler. 'It was as if never-heard, never-suspected secrets were being revealed. And then I saw him...'

Schindler also recalled the moment. The concert hall was filled to capacity, and Beethoven stood near the podium in the midst of the orchestra. He was conspicuous in his incongruous green frock coat – it was the only suitable one he owned – and he was lost in rapture. His love of and communion with nature, the ideals of enlightenment and freedom bred into him – all in opposition to the suffering and pain which had suffused his life; the pain of his own father reeling drunken through the streets and physically abusing him – all were triumphing now, in the end, with the composition of a symphony that was an affirmation of mankind, of brotherhood in the face of war and destruction and an answer to all forms of human pettiness.

'Do you remember the thunderous applause?' asked Johanna.

'Yes, of course.'

The audience, which listened with pure attention, burst several times into ovation. At the entrance of the kettledrum *timpani* into the frolicsome *scherzo* during the second movement, their applause returned in a thunderous, volcanic eruption. Beethoven, his back turned to the audience, heard nothing. And the shock of this recognition, that he had heard nothing, had an electric effect on the audience. Men threw their hats

into the air, women waved scarves and handkerchiefs –
all to show the appreciation and adulation that could
not be shared by applause alone. Then something
prompted him to turn around.

He bowed, solemnly, abruptly, ungraciously – and yet
beautifully.

'The ovation seemed as it would never end,' said
Schindler.

'And then,' said Johanna, her eyes shining, remembering, 'he saw me ... There were all those people in the
concert hall,' she paused for a moment, choked up, tears
welling in her eyes, 'and it was as if we were alone.'

And then Johanna told Schindler what followed.

As he lay dying, the master sent for her. She did not
know whether she ought to go and decided against it
several times, but finally she could not stay away. At
the Schwarzspanierhaus, she met Beethoven's brother
Johann and his wife Therese.

'His belly's swollen with dropsy,' said Therese. 'Five
times the surgeons have made a puncture to drain off
the fluid. The incisions have become inflamed. His
strength is now gone and I fear the death-struggle is
approaching.'

Johanna said nothing. She looked towards
Beethoven's bedroom, wanting to enter, to be with
him, alone, for the last time.

Johann's monocle fell from his eye. 'I want him to
receive last rites while he's still conscious. But this
afternoon when I suggested to send for a priest, he
turned his face to the wall and called me an ass.'

'Not unusual for him,' said Therese.

'But then he asked for you,' said Johann, turning to
Johanna, looking at her closely. 'I don't know why.' He

shook his head as though in wonder. 'My brother is dying. Soon he will be gone from this earth.'

Johanna quietly stepped into the darkened bedroom. The curtains were drawn and the bright sunshine of early spring scarcely penetrated the gloom. Beethoven was propped up in bed. His appearance was shocking. He was emaciated and jaundiced, his flesh drawn and cracked like old paper. Only his eyes, although darkly ringed, were still striking. His abdomen was bandaged from the dropsy and the drainings.

'On his lap was music paper,' said Johanna, with a glance at Schindler, but an inward glance as though she were talking to herself.

'He was writing the Cavatina of the Galitsin, one of the last string quartets.'

Beethoven laid down his pen and held out a hand. She hesitated, then crossed the room and took his hand in both of hers. They sat looking at each other and said nothing.

'We needed no words,' said Johanna. 'We had gone far beyond words. He handed me a paper relinquishing guardianship over Karl.'

He then tried to smile, and atop the score of the Cavatina, he scrawled, in nearly illegible hand:

Must it be?

She wrote in return, *'It must be.'*

Beethoven read her reply, engaged her eyes, and said, *'Plaudite, amici, comoedia finita est.'*

Applaud, friends, for the comedy has ended.

It was the death of Beethoven as Schindler also remembered it. There was no question but that she was telling the truth. But then he realized, with a sense of shock, that the larger truth eluded her when she said to him, 'Yes, I loved him once. I loved him and he turned his back on me. I was a fool. I never meant anything to him.'

'But the letter, Frau Beethoven. What about the letter?'

Johanna looked into his eyes, her own wide with apprehension and confusion.

'What letter?' she asked.

Chapter 19

Return to Karlsbad

Schindler, trying with little success to hide his misery, handed the letter to the Immortal Beloved to Johanna, saying, 'I believe this was addressed to you. It would perhaps be better if you were alone now.' He then bowed and walked out of the door. As he passed in front of the store he could see the women inside busy, at their labours. He looked up and saw a flock of gulls, and heard – for now it was spring – nuthatches hidden in the trees. He turned and gazed once more at Johanna through the shop window.

My angel, my all, my other self, just a few words today and that in pencil (yours) . . .

She stood quite still, reading the letter. Her mouth was twisted in sorrow as tears flooded her cheeks.

Schindler turned away.

He took the next coach to Karlsbad.

My journey was a fearful one; I did not reach here until four o'clock yesterday morning. Lacking horses the postcoach chose another route, but what an awful one; at the stage before the last I was warned not to travel at night; I was made fearful of a forest, but that only made me the more eager – and I was wrong. The coach must needs break down on the wretched road, a bottomless mud rood...

On his way to Karlsbad, Schindler began to understand what had so long eluded him. The master had written in letters, *I am the real, corporeal father of Karl*. Always until now Schindler had put that down to the transcendence, and perhaps the unreliability, of deep emotion. But who was to say...? Beethoven and Johanna *had* been in love; Schindler had been able to read that love clearly on Johanna's face. She *had*, after all, journeyed to Karlsbad to await him on that long ago day in July of 1806. And if they had loved each other, which seemed clear to Schindler now, and they were both young and passionate, that love surely must have shown itself.

Karl had been born seven months after they had arranged to meet in Karlsbad. Had she whispered it to him? That was the question for the ages.

I am the real, corporeal father of Karl...

Schindler's thoughts were deep as the coach drew near Karlsbad. Only one person, Johanna, could answer that riddle for certain, and Schindler knew that it was a secret, assuming it was true, that she would carry to her grave.

* * *

'So you're back,' said Frau Streicher when he reached the Swan Hotel.

'Yes, I am back,' said Schindler.

'To stay a while, I hope. The baths are good this time of year. Good for your health.'

'I am sure that they are,' said Schindler. 'But for the moment, I would just like to see the room.'

'The room. You've seen it already, haven't you?'

'I need to see it again,' said Schindler.

Frau Streicher was not happy to be inconvenienced for no good reason, but what could be done with a gentleman except to accommodate him? She led the way up the stairs and stood at the door, refusing to leave him alone.

'I hope *you* don't cause a ruckus.' She was slightly piqued by his lack of attention to her.

Schindler strode to the window, which looked out on to the court. 'That day we spoke about, Frau Streicher.'

She said, 'Don't remind me. It was a day I try to forget.'

'You received the letter and came up, knocked and brought in the tray of food. And the letter you had opened was on it.'

'Not exactly *opened*, Herr Schindler. It was addressed to the room, but as Beethoven was not here, I—'

'The letter was on the tray.'

'Why, yes,' said Frau Streicher. 'Beneath the teacup.'

'And she left soon after,' said Schindler.

'That's right.'

'And moments later, he arrived.'

'A very short time.'

'How much later, would you say?'

'Minutes, perhaps. Not more than minutes. She was gone, he was here. It happened that way. As though all at once.'

Yes, Schindler fathomed it all now. He gazed out of the window to where the coaches halted before the entrance to the hotel. He could see Johanna running down the stairs, mortified, certain that Beethoven had had a last-minute change of mind. Perhaps fearful of taking responsibility for the child she carried. He could see Beethoven arriving in his coach just as hers left, running through the lobby of the hotel, rushing up the stairs. To find her gone. To find the letter – undiscovered – there on the tray. His world smashed to bits.

But even though he understood it, perhaps he did not want to. The implications were highly disturbing. He would have to sort them out. He was thinking not so much of the truth of this episode in the master's life, of the truth of his own quest to find the Immortal Beloved, but of Beethoven's place in history. That they had loved each other Schindler had not a doubt; that the love that had come to pass between them was dark and catastrophic was clear to him.

He remembered these words from the letter:

While still in bed my thoughts turn to you, my Immortal Beloved, some of them happy, some sad, waiting to see whether fate will hear us.

And fate, Schindler thought as he boarded the coach for his return to Vienna, had not heard them.

Chapter 20

Finale

Anton Schindler ultimately recoiled, as well he might in the age in which he lived, from the notion that Johanna was the Immortal Beloved. He suppressed evidence of her appearance at Beethoven's deathbed, and later criticized her much as he pilloried all the other members of the composer's family. He could not countenance the idea that the two brothers had loved and possessed the same woman. Much less could he accept the possibility that Beethoven was, as he once expressed it, the 'real, corporeal father of Karl'.

In 1840, Schindler wrote a hasty biography of Beethoven, a task which fell to him by default, and for which he was not highly suited. That was when he revealed the existence of the letter to the Immortal Beloved, which immediately came to occupy its central place in Beethoven's life story. Schindler himself assigned the identity of the unknown woman to Countess Giucciardi. No one believed him, then or

213

since. Schindler died, quite an old man for those days, in 1864.

Karl Beethoven pursued a career as a soldier, and later as a private citizen in Vienna. He married and was reported to be a good husband and father to four daughters. He died in 1858.

Johanna, after Beethoven's death, did indeed regain without opposition guardianship of her son Karl, whom she outlived by a decade. She died in Baden, impoverished, at the age of eighty-two. Rumours of a relationship between Johanna and Beethoven, which started up after her death, were taken to be ungrounded. She was never acknowledged as the Immortal Beloved.

In 1888, the body of Ludwig van Beethoven was removed from the outskirts of Vienna and reburied in the city's Central Cemetery. There he rests today, and his gravesite is visited by many who pass through Vienna, by those who possess, in addition to love for his music, a fragment of human compassion, wrought from life, for the man who wrote, Eternally yours, Eternally mine, Eternally we.

More Enchanting Fiction from Headline

JOANNA McDONALD
ISLAND GAMES

EVERYTHING YOU THINK YOU WANT IS YOURS – AT A PRICE

Nell McLean couldn't be less like her twin brother Tally. He is tall and slim with predatory sex appeal, while she has put pasta before passion and developed into dress size 'large'. He has a series of glamorous, gossip-column girlfriends while she has lots of good friends for platonic gossip. Neither is content.

The twin turning point comes when Tally tires of girls who dine on herbal tea and vitamin C and Nell gets sick of watching other people dieting at her dinner parties. They quit the capital and answer the call of their Scottish roots, turning a dilapidated castle on a beautiful Hebridean island into a low-fat, high-luxury haven for exhausted jet-setters and tired tycoons. An island paradise to revive the most jaded of appetites – and not only for healthy food…

Just as the visiting guests succumb to the sensual charm of Taliska so it works its magic on the twins, giving each of them what they think they most desire. Tally finds true love with an appetite and Nell finds sex and a sylph-like figure – but at what cost to each?

With wry humour and bittersweet accuracy, ISLAND GAMES is for anyone who ever laughed, loved or wanted to be someone else.

FICTION/GENERAL   0 7472 4546 0

BID TIME RETURN

THE COMPULSIVE SAGA OF A FAMILY
HAUNTED BY THE TRAGIC PAST

DONNA BAKER

AUTHOR OF
THE WEAVER'S GLORY

LOUISA

The daughter of a wealthy ironmaster, her life is changed for ever when her father remarries. Made to feel unwanted in her home, she takes refuge in the company of gypsies; more than anything she envies their freedom.

RUPERT

Barely eleven when his father marries Elinor, he scarcely knows what a mother is. His father rarely mentions her and when he does it is with a bitterness that implies Rupert and his mother were accomplices in a crime against him. But what it could be, Rupert has no idea – until his stepmother seduces him.

JOANNA

An orphan, she has come to Furness to seek her family and finds she has inherited more than a house and mining business. Determined to unravel the tainted and tangled past, Joanna discovers a tragic pattern of relationships from one generation to the next. A pattern that is in danger of being repeated...

Don't miss Donna Baker's previous novels, also available from Headline: THE WEAVER'S DAUGHTER, THE WEAVER'S DREAM and THE WEAVER'S GLORY – 'a nicely judged mixture of love and politics' (Netta Martin, *Annabel*); and CRYSTAL, BLACK CAMEO and CHALICE – 'a good family storyline, lots of atmosphere and strong love' *(Woman's World)*, 'captures the imagination' *(Best)*.

FICTION/SAGA   0 7472 4325 5

A selection of bestsellers
from Headline

THE CHANGING ROOM	Margaret Bard	£5.99 ☐
BACKSTREET CHILD	Harry Bowling	£5.99 ☐
A HIDDEN BEAUTY	Tessa Barclay	£5.99 ☐
A HANDFUL OF HAPPINESS	Evelyn Hood	£5.99 ☐
THE SCENT OF MAY	Sue Sully	£5.99 ☐
HEARTSEASE	T R Wilson	£5.99 ☐
NOBODY'S DARLING	Josephine Cox	£5.99 ☐
A CHILD OF SECRETS	Mary Mackie	£5.99 ☐
WHITECHAPEL GIRL	Gilda O'Neill	£5.99 ☐
BID TIME RETURN	Donna Baker	£5.99 ☐
THE LADIES OF BEVERLEY HILLS	Sharleen Cooper Cohen	£5.99 ☐
THE OLD GIRL NETWORK	Catherine Alliott	£4.99 ☐

*All Headline books are available at your local bookshop or newsagent, or
can be ordered direct from the publisher. Just tick the titles you want and fill
in the form below. Prices and availability subject to change without notice.*

Headline Book Publishing, Cash Sales Department, Bookpoint, 39 Milton
Park, Abingdon, OXON, OX14 4TD, UK. If you have a credit card you may
order by telephone – 0235 400400.

Please enclose a cheque or postal order made payable to Bookpoint Ltd to the
value of the cover price and allow the following for postage and packing:
UK & BFPO: £1.00 for the first book, 50p for the second book and 30p for
each additional book ordered up to a maximum charge of £3.00.
OVERSEAS & EIRE: £2.00 for the first book, £1.00 for the second book and
50p for each additional book.

Name ....

Address ....

....

....

If you would prefer to pay by credit card, please complete:
Please debit my Visa/Access/Diner's Card/American Express (delete as
applicable) card no:

Signature .... Expiry Date ....